LAVINIA DERWENT

God Bless the Borders!

Illustrated by Elizabeth Haines

ARROW BOOKS

Also in Arrow by Lavinia Derwent

A BORDER BAIRN
A BREATH OF BORDER AIR
A MOUSE IN THE MANSE

Arrow Books Limited
62–65 Chandos Place, London WC2N 4NW

An imprint of Century Hutchinson Ltd.

London Melbourne Sydney Auckland
Johannesburg and agencies throughout
the world

First published by Hutchinson 1981

Arrow edition 1982
Reprinted 1982 and 1987

Printed and bound in Great Britain
by Anchor Brendon Ltd,
Tiptree, Essex

ISBN 0 09 928030 2

To Jethart

Contents

1. Uppies and Doonies

'I've lost yesterday,' I once wailed to Jessie when I was a child trying to recall some trivial happening of the day before. 'Where's it gone?'

'Hoots! it's still there in your heid. Think aboot it, lassie, an' it'll come back.'

I have taken Jessie's advice in this as in so many things. And when I think of yesterday it is her I see most clearly, close enough almost to clasp her work-roughened hand. A hand that could comfort or sting when she slapped me on the cheek for some misdeed. All for my own good. 'I'll mak' a wumman oot ye yet.'

But not a woman like herself. The pattern is unrepeatable. I trotted at her heels as a bairn and have tried to follow her footsteps ever since. She was the focal point of my early life. It was to her apron I clung for consolation, not expecting cuddles or kisses. Jessie had none to give, only cold common sense. Rummlegumption. But at least she listened to me when others were too preoccupied. And it was through her eyes I first saw the world.

God Bless the Borders!

The world was a rambling old farmhouse tucked away in the Border hills far from the main road. A world on its own. Our only neighbours were the farmworkers in the cottages. Hinds, they were called. And Jessie herself, who lived with her brother Jock-the-herd and her sister Joo-anne in the herd's hoose a short distance away. No passers-by, only the clopping carthorses or a tramp seeking shelter in the barn. Beyond lay the Cheviots leading to England, and above that the sky encompassing us all, Scots and Sassenachs.

The stone-flagged kitchen was Jessie's domain; mine, too, more than the parlour or any of the other rooms, upstairs or down. Here I could sit on the fireside rug, mindful of the black kettle spitting at me from the swey, a sickly lamb wrapped in a blanket beside me, a chick chirping its way back to life in the oven with a peep of heat left on, and feel part of the endless activity going on around me. Ironing, mangling, churning, jam-making, baking; the postie or the herd coming clattering in, and always Jessie there to say a word to me, if only, 'Get oot ma road, lassie.'

'Oot' meant out, and outside was even better than the kitchen, for there I had the run of the farmyard and a host of friends. The beasts. They were all part of the family. I felt as much related to the cows and collies, even to Grumphy, the pig, as I did to my parents.

I have only to smell a whiff of woodsmoke or hear a curlew call and the old blurred pictures come back into focus. Father yoking Flora, the pony, into the gig, Grumphy scratching his hairy back against a stucking-post, Jessie dunking a broody clocker in the water barrel, myself falling into the midden.

She was right, Jessie. Yesterday is never lost.

Town folk seemed to think I lived on a different planet. Away out in the country.

'Isn't it awful quiet?' they asked pityingly.

'No! Neither awful nor quiet.'

There is no absolute silence in the countryside. Nature never stays still. There is always some creature stirring, a tree sighing, a gate creaking, a cow coughing, a dog barking. Outdoor sounds are never completely switched off.

Far less the sounds in a shabby old farmhouse. At dead of night a wakerife bairn could lie and listen to the falling of ash in the grate, the groaning of a wardrobe, the scamper of mice feet in the garret above, the wheeze of a grandfather clock, the snoring of the kitchen lass in her narrow bed. Or the mad mutterings of Yorkie, the tramp, as he came rambling up the road in search of shelter.

Half awake, half asleep, I sometimes wondered where I was. Alive or dead? During the day I had no doubts. I lived at Overton Bush, Jedburgh, Roxburghshire, the World; but in the pitch darkness I fancied myself away in that Other Place waiting for the last trump to sound. In a panic I stretched out my hand to feel for the familiar candlestick on the bedside table. It was there! I could turn on my pillow and go safely to sleep, knowing I would rise from the dead in the morning.

I liked the early morning sounds best, when the household stirred and life-blood began to flow. Friendly sounds. The clatter of clogs on the stone kitchen floor, the rattle of a milk pail, the crowing of the banty cock, the herd's voice shouting to his collies, the tramp of the hinds' feet on their way round to the work stable.

Best of all, the birds, especially the blackies trilling the same phrase over and over again, then suddenly switching to a surprising variation. It was like listening to a concert, trying to guess the theme and wishing the birds would put words to their music. Scottish words? And would the blackbirds beyond the Carter Bar sing in a Geordie accent?

We had our own names in the Borders for the birds. The owl was the hoolet, the crow the corbie, the dove the cushy-doo, the chaffinch the shilfy, the lapwing the pees-

weep, the curlew the whaup, the linnet the linty, the
yellow-hammer the yellow-yite. The skylark – the
laverock – was my favourite.

We had learnt a poem about the skylark at school:

> Bird of the wilderness,
> Blithesome and cumberless. . . .

Never mind what cumberless meant. It was poetry and
flowed sweetly from one phrase to another as if the bird
itself was singing. And it had been written, not by the
prolific Anon, but by James Hogg, the Ettrick Shepherd.

A Border shepherd writing poetry! I took a closer look at
our own shepherd. If James Hogg could do it, why not
Jock-the-herd?

He was mending the wheelbarrow when I approached
him. Jock's main occupation was tending the beasts, but he
could turn his hand to a wide range of activities. Building
dykes, putting up henhouses, fixing barbed-wire fences,
killing pigs, calving cows, sweeping chimneys, clearing the
clogged kitchen sink, mending almost anything that was
broken. But maybe composing verses was beyond his skill.
Still, it was worth asking.

'Have you ever thought of writing poetry, Jock?'

He was accustomed to my daft questions and showed no
sign of surprise. Sometimes he did not even bother to
answer; but today, after knocking in a last nail, he straightened up and gave me a quizzical glance.

'Pottry! Canna stand it.'

'But do you know any, Jock?'

He considered for a moment. 'I ken "Baa-baa, black
sheep". Man-lassie, dinna sit doon in that barra. Ye're
gettin' ower big.'

I liked sitting in the barrow and sometimes Jock could be
coaxed to give me a hurl in it, but maybe I was getting too
big. All the same, I sat in it and continued the exploration of
Jock's mind. What a nuisance I must have been!

'What do you think about, Jock, when you're out on the hill?'

'Sheep.'

'Well, then! You could write a poem about sheep. Better than "Baa-baa, black sheep". Have you ever heard of the Ettrick Shepherd?'

'Ye mean Tod Tamson? I whiles meet him at the lamb sales.'

'No, no! This one's dead. He was a poet.' Eager to fill in the gap, I told him about James Hogg. 'He used to carry a little inkwell and a pen in his pocket when he was out on the hirsel; and whenever he had an inspiration he stopped and wrote down a poem. Would you like to hear one?'

'No!'

Nothing deterred, I launched into 'Bird of the wilderness. . . .'

'Man-lassie, get oot that barra.' Jock whistled to his dogs. 'Come on, Jed! Up, Jess! Time we were awa' roond the hill.'

Perhaps he would never be a poet but, as I watched him striding away with his crook in his hand and the dogs at his heels, it suddenly struck me that Jock-the-herd was a character. And that I was surrounded by characters, some more interesting than those in any storybooks. Jessie, Father, the postie, Auld Baldy-Heid, Bella at the shop, Dafty at the Grammar School, Yorkie the tramp. Nobody was just ordinary.

For all I knew, I was a character myself.

Life was all ups and downs, like the Border hills. Better that way than living on a level keel without even a small hummock to surmount. On my way to the village school I had to change gear constantly, so that I could scurry down the slopes and put in an extra spurt going up the steep braes.

'It tak's a stoot hert to a stey brae,' was an oft-quoted

saying. But the ups became downs on the way home, and the variety added spice to the journey.

The same with people. Miss Paleface, the English teacher at the Grammar School, was too even-tempered for my taste. 'Mim-mou'd', Jessie would have called her. Never flying into rages like Auld Baldy-Heid or Dafty. Yorkie the tramp, bellowing to the moon, often made my blood curdle, but his surprise visits to the farm shook us out of ourselves. Something unpredictable was happening.

The most unpredictable event in the Border calendar was Handba' Day, when the natives of Jedburgh were divided into Uppies and Doonies, depending on whether they lived above or below the marketplace. It was supposed to be a game, but one fought in such deadly earnest that strangers would have wondered if a war had broken out.

The very fact of separating themselves into Uppies and Doonies turned friendly neighbours into bitter rivals; and it was a mercy they had no ammunition other than fists and feet, else the High Street would have been littered with corpses. As it was, there were plenty of bleeding noses, black eyes and bandaged brows to be seen at the end of the contest.

Every shop was shut, every window boarded up to prevent the glass breaking, and the entire town turned into a battlefield. Traffic had to take a roundabout route to avoid the mêlée, with puzzled drivers asking, 'What's it all about?'

Not an easy question to answer. There were varied versions. Some said the handba' was an Englishman's head to be kicked around the streets as a defiant gesture to right old wrongs. But no one really cared about its origins. As long as the Uppies won. Or the Doonies.

It was a great way of settling private feuds. 'I'll sort *him* at the Handba'.'

It was mainly hims and not hers who took part in the fray, though the womenfolk sometimes stood on the sidelines, adding to the dirdum by shouting encouragement or abuse at the men.

'Watch oot, Geordie! There's the ba'. Get haud o't, man! Eediot! A Doonie's got it!'

It seemed a matter of life or death whether Uppies or Doonies won the day; and every single move was reported in an enlarged edition of the *Jethart Squeaker*.

The Uppies, in the shape of Mr J. Cowan, Castlegate, regained possession of the ball, but was instantly felled to the ground by Mr William Scott, Bongate, and sustained minor injuries. The Doonies then swept into the Wynd and tried to smuggle the ball, but were stopped by the Uppies who charged at them from all directions. A close battle then ensued. . . .

The reporter, poor man, was little more than a handball himself, forced to suffer blows from Uppies and Doonies alike, and sometimes sent flying through the air, still valiantly clutching his notebook.

The real handball was about the size of a tennis ball, bedecked at the outset with coloured ribbons soon to be torn to shreds. It was thrown up by the chief man in the town – the heid bummer – the provost, with great ceremony in the marketplace where throngs of Uppies and Doonies were waiting with upstretched hands to take possession of it as it fell down.

It was the first of several such balls, some eight or ten depending on how long a game took to reach its conclusion, all donated and thrown up by prominent members of the community. Names and addresses sedulously noted in the local paper.

If there were any rules, I never knew them. The main object was to score goals by conveying the balls, by fair means or foul, to their desinations. In the Doonies' case to a hiding place up near the castle, and in the Uppies' to a spot down near the Townfoot Brig. Though I never got the hang of the game, I always felt pleased when the Uppies won, for I supposed I came under that category, living as I did above and beyond the marketplace.

But it was not a game for girls. The big boys at school talked about it for weeks before and after, proudly displaying their scars and boasting of blows given or received. Only once was I marginally involved in the battle.

I had jinked away from parental control to follow the shouting mob up the High Street, and stood watching for a time in the shelter of a doorway, marvelling at the antics of the grown-ups. The same grown-ups who would take *me* to task if I became too high-spirited or let my hair get into a tousled tangle. There they were, in their oldest duds, dishevelled beyond recognition, grunting like wild beasts as they heaved against each other in their efforts to gain possession of the ball. No use calling out, 'Behave yourselves!' They were beyond behaving.

Suddenly I was aware of a wee man breaking away from the group and slinking stealthily towards me. He thrust something into my hand and hissed, 'Quick! Away an' smuggle it. Doon at the Brig! Go on!'

This was the great thing, to find a means of extracting the ball from the throng, and get someone to smuggle it secretly into its goal mouth. The ball was safely in my hand when the wee man was seized, and disappeared from sight in the thick of the fight, leaving me frozen like a statue, hiding the handball behind my back.

This could have been my hour of glory. Had I the nerve to wander casually away in the direction of the Townfoot Brig, deposit the ball and win a goal for the Uppies? The howling mob would show no mercy if they spotted me. They would pounce on me like terriers worrying a fox to death. Was it worth taking the risk?

Yes!

In a split second I made up my mind to go for glory. Think of the headlines in the *Squeaker*. They might even print my photograph.

BRAVE SCHOOLGIRL SCORES. . . .

It was not to be. Suddenly I was seized from behind by Mrs Veitch on whose doorstep I was standing.

'Fling it awa',' she ordered me urgently. 'Mercy! have ye nae sense? They'll murder ye! Fling it awa'.'

So I took the coward's way out and tossed the handball from me, whether to Uppies or Doonies I could not tell. Then I was hauled backwards into the house, and Mrs Veitch barred the door firmly against the mob.

I felt deflated. Proud, too, to think I had actually held the handba' even for such a brief moment. But it was frustrating, for the windows were shuttered, and there was no chance of keeking out to see how the battle was raging. Mrs Veitch insisted on making me a cup of tea and kept me sitting by the fireside till the din died in the distance.

'That's them awa' into the Jed,' she said as she let me out of the door. 'Daft deevils! they'll stop at naething.'

I knew her man was in the thick of the throng. Father, too, as I found out later on when I slunk down one of the wynds towards the river. There they were, splashing about in the water like children, drenched to the waist, heedless of the angry swans who had joined the fray and were pecking viciously at anyone within reach.

Daft deevils? Yes, but it was fun watching them let off steam. Better a bruised brow than one wrinkled with worry. Following the wavering fortunes of the game, I realized I was not alone in my ups and downs.

Anything but alone. For the highest power of all kept a watchful eye on the Borders.

What a relief it was on Sundays when we heard the minister asking God to bless us. It meant he was nearing the end of the lang prayer. He had droned on for ages, telling the almighty what sinners we were. Little wonder we bowed our heads in shame. We had lied, fornicated, coveted our neighbours' cattle and strayed from the paths of righteousness. I was thankful the minister did not know all my transgressions. My breaking the teapot spout, for example. But maybe He knew already. Thou, God, see-est me.

After flattening us into submission and asking for forgiveness, the minister prayed for the royal family, those who govern over us, the crops, and finally – oh! what a welcome word – 'And finally, God bless the Borders. Amen!'

Even with such an omnipotent ally, I still strayed into tortuous paths of wickedness; though usually, like the Grand Old Duke's men, I was only halfway up. Neither up nor down.

But I was one up on Jessie. For by now I had achieved enough self-assurance to speak back to her. No longer did I take her word for law.

'Losh, lassie! Ye'd argue with your shadow,' she grumbled at me.

Sometimes I won the battles, sometimes Jessie did. She was still my best friend, my mentor, my refuge in times of trouble. I think I grew fonder of her after finding out her flaws; but I would not give in if I thought I was right and she was wrong.

'It's your own fault, Jessie,' I told her. 'You were the one who taught me rummlegumption.'

'Huh! ye've got a lang road to gang yet, lassie.'

Maybe, but I had taken the first steps and I was on the right road.

2. Mud Student

The most familiar sight to any farm bairn is mud.

'Glaur' we called it in the Borders. When the glaur was wet and sticky it was described as being 'clatchy'. It clung to clogs and boots, it trailed its way into the house, it was, as Jessie said, a terrible slaister.

In rainy weather the entire farm became a quagmire. Jessie kilted up her long skirts as she tramped through it. The hinds and the herd tied thongs – called nicky-tams – round their trouser legs to keep their breeks from trailing in the dirt. Even so, they were often bespattered. It was part of their trademark.

It did not matter much to me if I was running barefoot. The burn was nearby and I could dabble in it like a duck before entering the house. There was a scraper, a rough mat, and a stout brush – a bussm – outside the kitchen door.

'Dicht your feet!' Jessie would yell when she heard any-one approaching.

There was a conglomeration of old boots under the

kitchen table. Communal footgear caked with mud. It was a case of help yourself and never mind whether they fitted or not. Often I went clumping about in outsize boots, sometimes stepping out of one and leaving it stuck in a mound of mud. But it was no use turning up our noses at the glaur. It was just something we lived with. Good clean dirt.

The beasts took it for granted. Grumphy the sow wallowed in it, grunting sensuously as she rolled over and over till covered from snout to tail, Her mudbath seemed to give her great satisfaction, though it did not improve her looks. The cocks and hens pecked happily in it. It was only the cats who tried to avoid it, stepping with dainty feet on to any clean surface they could find.

'Ay, ye micht lairn a lesson frae *them*,' Jessie suggested, but it was easier just to splash through the glaur and take the consequences. And if one was half-dirty, what was the odds? One might as well become whole-dirty.

Sometimes I had to carry a pail of warm water round to the byre so that Jessie could wash the cows' udders before starting the milking. I had given up worrying about the beasts standing out in the fields in wet weather suffering from rheumatism or catching influenza. Though when I heard a sheep coughing – cough-cough-cough, like a child with whooping cough – I felt sorry for the poor creature. Jock-the-herd doctored the sick with doses from the bottles he kept in the bothy, and in drastic cases Father sent for the vet. But mostly they remained healthy. Beasts and humans alike, we thrived on fresh air and mud.

After a downpour it was exciting to see the burn in spate, with the frothy water swirling round the stepping-stones, sweeping everything downstream. Empty lemonade bottles, cocoa tins, broken pans and pails, all sent on a journey to an unknown destination. Would they all reach the sea, maybe, and end up on a foreign shore?

The fields were often like swamps; yet in due course

everything grew and flourished. I never questioned how or why. Maybe it was something to do with the minister praying to the Great Farmer in the sky, though the Lord did not always oblige by providing the right kind of weather to suit everyone. Tilling the soil was a ticklish job, depending not only on the skills of the farmers and the vagaries of the climate. Instinct played a large part in the successful running of a farm; but it was a hitty-missy process at the best of times.

None of the neighbouring farmers I knew had been to agricultural colleges. They had just followed in their fathers' footsteps, gaining practical experience as laddies by jumping on to reapers, stooking corn, and helping the shepherd at the lambing.

Fine for farmers' sons who could practise on their own land; but there were other youths with no country connections who wanted to learn the trade. How could they find out? Requests would sometimes come from parents anxious to get their sons placed on a farm as extra hands so that they could learn by experience, by being taken on as apprentices.

Mud students they were called in the Borders.

They found it hard going, these town-bred lads with no notion of country ways. It was not easy keeping up with the hinds who treated them as 'orra-men' – odd-job workers fit only for the most menial tasks. They were made to spread dung, clean out the pigsty, dig drains, and trudge over rough braes rounding up stray sheep till the poor things were ready to drop in their tracks. It was the survival of the fittest.

Those who were made of the right stuff soon lost their city pallor, broadened out and developed enormous appetites. As well as Border accents. Soon they were discussing the rotation of crops as to the manner born. Others who were less robust fell by the wayside and, having got farming out of their systems, scuttled back home to more restful jobs as bank clerks, thankful to leave their muddy boots behind.

Father never took on a mud student, but at one time a young lad came to us daily, not so much to learn the outs and ins of farming as to benefit his health by being out in the fresh air. Jessie called him 'the Callant', and had a soft spot for him because he looked so peely-wally. He seemed a carefree character to me, and never mentioned his ailments or his future plans. I think he already knew there would be no future for him.

The Callant was the brother of my first friend, Gwen, who had died of a decline. He had the same cough, the same weakness in his chest, the same look of being somewhere else. His parents dreaded he had the same disease, as indeed he had. So his father, factor to the laird's estate, asked if he could come as a kind of honorary mud student and have the freedom of the farm.

Soon the Callant became as familiar a figure as a tattie-bogle or a haystack. Every day when he was well enough he walked up from the factor's house at Camptown and sat dangling his legs on the dyke, riding one of the workhorses or daundering round with Jock-the-herd. The men tolerated him, and Jessie tried to fatten him up as if he was going to the sales.

To this end, she forced him to drink vast tumblers of frothy milk straight from the cow. No doubt the worst thing for him. All the milk at that time was untested, so it was little wonder so many farm bairns suffered from consumption in one form or another.

I hardly noticed the Callant, except to keep out of his way. He was older than my age group for one thing. For another, he had a mocking wit which I did not know what to make of, and a disconcerting habit of never addressing me directly. There was always an invisible third person present with whom he discussed my shortcomings. He had discovered plenty of *them*.

The best I could do was take avoiding action. I climbed fences and skirted round fields to keep out of range of his teasing tongue.

'See her!' he would say to the unseen somebody. 'What's she up to now? She'll get stuck on the barbed wire. Serve her right if she comes a cropper. Look at her hair! What a ticket!'

The Callant did his best to irritate me; yet I felt sorry for him, but how could I express it? He was not sorry for himself. He loved riding the workhorses, perhaps seeing himself as a robust cowboy. Flora, the pony, came trotting to his call. Even the cross bubblyjock made friends with him.

'That Callant's got a way wi' beasts,' said Jessie.

Not only beasts. He would catch her round the waist and give her a hug, a thing I never dared do. 'Daft article!' she would remonstrate, but she never boxed his ears or gave him the rough side of her tongue. She knitted him a long gravat, and was for ever handing him out wee bites to fill up the corners. The Callant always accepted them, but I sometimes saw him passing on the offerings to the hens or the pigs.

The Boss and the Callant got on a treat, but then all the workers got on well with Father. Still, the Callant had more privileges than most. The rare privilege, for example, of being invited into that holy of holies, the greenhouse. There he and Father took shelter together in showery weather. I could see them through the glass windows in animated conversation. What were they talking about? Not the running of the farm, I felt sure. They seemed to laugh too much for that.

Father taught the Callant to play the tin whistle. Often I heard the strains of 'Little Brown Jug' or 'The Keel Row'. They would sit there for ages on upturned pails, like a couple of schoolboys, long after the shower had passed and the sun was streaming in.

I grew so accustomed to the Callant that I seldom noticed his absence or presence. That was why I got such a shock of surprise on the day I was sent to the greenhouse with a message for Father.

'The tellyphone wants the Boss. It's the sheep-dip man,' said Jessie who had unwillingly answered the call. 'Haud on!' she had bawled down the receiver. 'He's oot!'

I ran up to the greenhouse to relay the message. Father and the Callant were absorbed in a game of draughts. It seemed a shame to disturb them, but I had to knock on the door. Father looked up at me as if he had never set eyes on me before.

'Sheep-dip!' he grunted, making it sound like a bad word, and reluctantly rose to answer the summons.

I was about to follow him when I heard the Callant speaking. Not to me but to the third person.

'What's her hurry? Silly thing! Can she not stop and hear what I have to say?'

I turned on my tracks and said impatiently, 'What is't?' Something sarcastic, likely, about my appearance. I knew there was a smudge of ink on my nose, for I had been helping Liz-Ann, the Carthorse, to pen a letter to her lad, George.

The Callant had not noticed the smudge. He did not look directly at me but got out his pocket-knife and began paring away at a seedbox. I could see he was embarrassed. So was I, wondering what was coming.

He took his time, then spoke casually. 'So my mother said you'd better ask that daft lassie to your birthday party.'

'What?'

I caught my breath in surprise. Fancy the Callant asking *me* to a party, even in such a roundabout way.

'She can come if she likes,' he said, turning away. 'It's at six o'clock on Friday. And if she doesn't like, it's no loss.'

'I'll see,' I said in a daze; but I knew I would go.

It was to be the Callant's last birthday party. A kind of

farewell. His parents had gathered together all his friends in the neighbourhood, so there was a motley mixture of age groups from me to Mary-Anne, with Big Bob, the gamey, and the minister in between. Even Auld Baldy-Heid, who had been the Callant's teacher for some time, was there, looking more human than usual.

The Callant paid no particular attention to me. Why should he with so many other folk there? My problem had been what to give him as a birthday present. Always low in funds, the most I could scrape together was sixpence. I knew if I asked Father he would dip his hand in his pocket. The Boss was a giver, but I was not an asker. Besides, I felt the Callant's present must come from *me,* so I had to do the best I could with my own sixpence.

I finally made my purchase from a tramp who called at the kitchen door with a shabby portmanteau which he opened out so that I could see the wonders if contained. Tawdry lace, ribbons, papers of pins and needles, combs, hair clasps. Nothing that could interest the Callant. Except for one item. A miniature mouth-organ, small enough to swallow.

'How much?' I asked the man.

'Two bob.'

He might as well have said a million pounds.

'I've only got sixpence,' I said and turned away. Whereupon he called me back and said craftily, 'It's yours for sixpence, lass, if ye can find me a pair o' auld troosers.'

I hoped Father would not miss the corduroy breeks I found in the back of the press. They were long past their best, with a patch on the seat and one leg shorter than the other, but the tramp accepted them readily enough, without looking for flaws.

The Callant never thanked me for the mouth-organ, but he used to go about the farmyard with it hidden in his mouth, blowing in-out in-out as if he was a bird whistling.

As for the party, I can recall little about it, except that we had a great spread, from hot pies to shivery jellies, and afterwards played games. It seemed strange to be Passing the Parcel to the minister and partnering the gamey at the 'Grand Old Duke of York'. Mary-Anne half sung, half recited an epic about an old maid in a garret, then someone suggested Postman's Knock.

I thought this a daft game, since our own postie never bothered to knock at the door. I had not played it before and was not acquainted with the rules, if any. The one time I was called out of the room was with Big Bob. We just stood in the lobby scowling at each other and then went back inside again.

The Callant's colour grew higher as the night wore on. His mother watched him anxiously when he took a fit of coughing and had to retire to the kitchen. But he was soon back again, determined to make things go with a swing; and, when we toasted him in lemonade and home-made wine, he pulled himself up, trying to look as hearty as possible.

Yet, though there was a good deal of merriment, I remember it as a sad evening, full of foreboding.

The Callant kept coming to the farm but more sporadically. Sometimes a week would pass without him turning up at all. Then Jessie would sigh and say, 'I doot he's bad.'

One day Father answered the telephone. He looked tight-lipped when he came through to the kitchen.

'The Callant'll not be coming back,' he said and went and shut himself in the greenhouse.

I remember another laddie – a real mud student – who stayed for some time on a neighbouring farm. Somehow I felt sorrier for him than for the Callant, though *he* was bouncing with health. Bouncing with self-confidence, too. He came from across the Border and spoke in what Jessie called a foreign accent. English.

'Guidness kens what he's supposed to be lairnin',' she sniffed. 'He thinks he's got it a' in his heid already.'

It was Dick's downfall. He was a know-all, full of himself and his own opinions. When he came to visit us with the Scotts he joined in the men's farming talk as if he was an old hand at the game. *He* knew when the corn should be cut, how it should be stooked, and when it was time to start the leading-in.

Mr Scott used to take a rise out of him. 'Och ay! he's a smart chap, Dick,' he would say, with a wink to my father. 'Dinna ken how I managed to run the farm before *he* came. He's got opeenions aboot everything.'

It was just as well Dick was not sensitive. The sarcasm stotted off his back. I was the one who felt embarrassed for his sake and would have sprung to his defence, had I dared.

'Why shouldn't he have opinions? You've got them. *We*'ve listened to yours, so give Dick a chance. Fair's fair.'

I never said it, of course.

I was often fed up with Dick myself. Sometimes we were sent out to look for eggs or to bring in the cows. Anything to get us out of the way. Then Dick could show off his superiority. He knew where the hens were likely to lay and the best tactics to use with the cows. I just let him sound off and said 'Uh-huh!' now and again, so he grew even bigger in his own estimation.

But sometimes the real boy would come through, and I sensed he was homesick for his family across the Border. He often spoke to me about his parents and about his little sister, Madge.

'She's like you,' he once told me. 'Only nicer.'

Well, at least, he did not stoop to flattery.

There was no need to press food on Dick as we had done with the Callant. A bottomless pit, Jessie called him. At teatime he scoffed up everything that was offered him and still looked for more.

'Dodsakes! ye'd think we starved him,' said the Scotts, well known in the district for keeping a good table themselves.

'At least he appreciates my baking,' said Mother mildly, and passed Dick the last slice of her sponge cake.

Then the silly laddie would spoil it all by telling her tactlessly what a good baker his mother was. 'You should taste *her* sponges. Light as a feather.'

He was his own worst enemy, Dick.

Yet he worked with a will for the Scotts and took a real interest in the running of the farm. No doubt he was smart enough to become minister of agriculture. Maybe he did. But when he left at the end of his term, Mr Scott sighed with relief.

'Jings! it's great to get rid o' that expert. I'll just muddle along in my own way. No more mud students for me.'

The hinds, I suppose, were the real mud students on our farm, though there was little left for *them* to learn. Who had taught them in the first place? Not Father, who was no dedicated farmer, but relied on them for the day-to-day running of the place, taking their advice at every turn; and somehow the work got done without any orders being issued.

But one dreaded job he had to tackle on his own was doing his accounts, sometimes in the greenhouse, sometimes at the big desk in the dining room where he sat groaning and ruffling his hair. I wished I could ease his burden, but I was no great shakes at sums myself. The sessions never lasted long. Suddenly he would open a drawer and take out an ocarino or a jew's harp, then play himself into oblivion. Father was a great one for dodging difficulties.

He was at his best when, having yoked the pony or cranked up the motor, he set off down the road away from the humdrum farm, out into the bigger world. The wives at the cottage always came out to wave as he passed by, and he never failed to touch his hat to them. Bowler, bonnet, straw basher, sometimes a lum hat. It was a highlight for them if the temperamental Tin Lizzie forced him to stop at their door.

'I had the Boss in for a kettle o' waitter to fill up the motor. Gied him a cup o' tea an' a bit gingerbreid. Sat doon in Tam's chair an' cracked awa', quite jacko.'

I can imagine how impatient Father would be to get away from Mrs Thing's clutches, but he would not have the heart to refuse her hospitality.

I sometimes wondered if Tam or Wull had ever wanted to be anything else but farmworkers. It was not easy to find out, or indeed to hold any conversations with them. Not just because they were inarticulate – they both had dry wits which surfaced now and again – but because they considered my questions too silly to answer.

All the same I tried one day while watching them curry-combing the Clydesdales in the work stable.

'Did you ever want to be anything else but hinds?'

Wull had paused to light his pipe. 'Ay,' said he, 'I've whiles fancied being a peony rose.'

Tam let out a strangled sound, the nearest he ever came to a laugh, and tried to cap his companion.

'I've aye had a notion to be the laird at the big hoose.' He had a shot at imitating the laird's English accent. 'Isn't this wondawful weathaw we're heving, doncha know?'

It was a good enough effort to cause Wull to choke on his pipe.

But it did not answer my question, so I gave it up.

3. Comers and Goers

'Michty God!' cried Jessie. 'Wha's ringing' the doorbell?'

It was the first time I had heard her give vent to such a strong expletive, and it startled me almost as much as the sudden clanging that echoed through the house.

On the rare occasions when the front doorbell rang it could only mean that gentry had arrived. Unexpected gentry at that. Otherwise Bella at the post office, our warning system, would have tipped us the wink.

'Watch oot!' she would shout down the telephone. Bella, I often thought, hardly needed a telephone. We might have heard her from Camptown, a mile away, without its aid. 'The meenister's on his way up to see ye.' Or, 'That's the Maiden Ladies oot for a wee hurl. They'll maybe pay ye a surprise veesit, so ye'd better get the kettle on, an' thraw up a scone.'

Scones were never baked, according to Bella, always thrown. And indeed we had to throw flour into the baking bowl and scones on to the girdle in our haste to be prepared for the surprise visitors. By the time they arrived there would be pancakes and toddies cooling on a wire tray on the kitchen table, maybe a gingerbread in the oven, and a fancy traycloth looked out.

If there was time my job – and a 'fikey' one it was, too – was to make wee butter balls for the gentry to spread on their dropscones. This involved dipping two wooden bats into boiling water and rolling the the butter round and round into little balls or curls. Then I would be sent to the jam cupboard and have to stand on a chair to pick out a jar of the best strawberry, kept for such special occasions.

Other callers, whether expected or not, would come and rap at the kitchen door or just walk in. The tramps, particularly Yorkie, would lift the sneck and shout to announce their presence.

'I'm here, missis! Can ye spare a bite to eat?' We never locked the doors, but we kept them shut, otherwise the cocks and hens, even Grumphy the pig would wander in. But certainly no tramp would ever dream of coming to the front door and ringing the bell.

'Michty God!' repeated Jessie when it gave another loud jangle. 'Ye'll need to gang, lassie. I'm up to the elbows.'

So she was.

We were alone in the house. Father and Mother had gone off on a jaunt to the other farm at Swinside, leaving me to help Jessie with the 'kirning' – the churning.

It was like taking part in a ritual. There was a right and a wrong time for catching the cream before it became curdled. 'Lappered' was Jessie's word for it. In thundery weather the cream turned quickly, so it had to be caught at the crucial moment.

The creaming-off took place in the milk-hoose, the coolest little room off the kitchen, where the milk had been settling in shallow dishes, waiting till the cream gathered. I liked the way it wrinkled when Jessie drew it to the side of the dish, with the big perforated ladle, before lifting it out and carefully conveying it to the earthenware crock to be added to yesterday's cream.

The clumsy wooden churn had been thoroughly cleansed and was set up in the middle of the kitchen with a stool at its side. Once the cream had been poured in and the bung securely fixed, I would sit on the stool and Jessie would say, 'Ca' canny at the start or it'll lapper.'

I knew better than to hurry. It was a hard job turning the heavy handle, and there was a knack of getting into the right rhythm. A slow hymn tune was the best. 'Rock of ages, cleft for me.' Or, 'Oh where, tell me where, has my Highland laddie gone?'

Jessie and I took turns to relieve the strain on the arms, then she would say, 'Speed up a bit, lassie! It's comin'!'

So I would change to 'Glory, glory, hallelujah!' turning the handle faster till we heard the welcome thud-thud and knew the butter had come.

'Stop!' Jessie would shout, catching at my arm. Then she turned the kirn round so that the bung was at the top, before unplugging it to peer inside at the butter. A sigh of relief. 'Ay! that's it!'

We both felt a sense of achievement and mentally shook hands, though the operation was far from finished.

I liked the next stage, for I got a glass of buttermilk. Soor dook. Jessie drained it off into a large bowl while I ran to fetch a tumbler. The soor dook had a bitter, yet refreshing taste, and left a white moustache on my mouth. If she was not bothered with the bile, Jessie might take a sip herself out of a cup; and we stood there drinking, taking our ease for a moment.

Not for long. When all the buttermilk was drained, Jessie whirled the churn right way up, rolled her sleeves well above the elbow and plunged in her hand to extract the butter. Not the moment to be interrupted by door-bells.

'Go on, lassie. Awa' an' answer it,' Jessie ordered me. 'An' wipe aff your moustache. Losh! I hope it's no' the laird.'

I paled at the thought as I went through the hall to the front door, hastily wiping off my moustache and trying to tidy my hair. I had no idea whom I was going to see on the doorstep, but my first reaction was relief. It was not the laird.

Was that a man or a boy? He had bare knees, short trousers, and was carrying a strange bundle on his back. Then I noticed he had a dark moustache, and wondered why a fully grown man was going about with bare knees, dressed in boy's trousers. He was not a tramp, surely; his clothes were neither ragged nor dirty.

He was mopping his brow when I opened the door.

'Excuse me,' he said politely, touching the woolly toorie he was wearing on his head. 'I wonder if you can help me?'

What could he be begging for? He did not look the kind who would want to sleep in the byre or in one of the outhouses. Perhaps he wanted a meal of bread and cheese.

'I'm looking for a route across the hills to the Carter Bar,' he said, slinging off his bundle. It was a kind of outsize schoolbag, a rucksack, from which he extracted a map. Unfolding it, he spread it out against the garden dyke.

It was a different kind of map from the atlas we used at school where we always seemed to be looking for the Mississippi river or Pernambuco, never anywhere nearby.

This had every local landmark on it, even our own farm. Fancy! Overton Bush, for all the world to see. The river Jed, Camptown, Edgerston. They were all there, looking every bit as important as Pernambuco.

'So if I go through that wood there, where would I get to?' the stranger was asking me.

To my hill with the castle on it. It, too, was marked on

the map. I traced out the route for him with my finger; but when he studied the scale and wondered how many miles it was, I was stumped. I had done it many a time myself, but miles were difficult to calculate. I just kept on walking till I got there.

'You could go down to the main road and maybe get a lift,' I suggested, fearing the route might be too long and rough for him.

No! That was not what he wanted, he told me, folding up his map.

'I'm hiking. Out walking.'

Hiking! It was a new word to me. I hiked all the time, I suppose, but always with a purpose: to get to the school, or the church, or to Camptown to buy something at Bella's shop. Not just out walking.

He had not asked for anything but, when he fastened on his rucksack and gave another mop to his brow, I suddenly said, 'Would you like a drink of soor dook?' I knew there was some left.

'Soor dook?'

'Buttermilk,' I explained and ran to fetch him a glass which he drank thankfully enough, leaning against the dyke. Then he said, 'Most refreshing, thank you,' and went off, having added a white moustache to his black one.

He was the first of the new breed of hikers who came, not exactly in droves, but in dribbles, till we grew accustomed to the doorbell ringing and strangers climbing over fences or struggling with the fastenings of a gate.

'Shut that yett!' Jock-the-herd called after them. He hated the hikers. 'I'll wring their necks,' he threatened when he found they had carelessly let the cows out of a field, or that Flora the pony had escaped and was nibbling the hollyhocks in the front garden. 'I've a guid mind to set the bull on them. They're aff their heids. Huh! ye wadna get me gaun for a hike.' This from Jock who walked dozens of miles a day and thought nothing of it.

I did not mind the hikers – they were new faces to read – as long as they kept away from my castle on the hill. I sometimes set them on their way by a roundabout route so that they would bypass my fortress. 'It's a short cut,' I said, telling a black lie, and they never knew the difference.

Father, too, took a lenient view of the intruders and could sometimes be seen showing off his sweetpeas to a stranger in shorts, or even inviting him into the greenhouse. The tramps had the freedom of the farm. Why not the hikers?

They, the tramps, were puzzled when they encountered such well-dressed wanderers, and looked at them suspiciously; but, when they discovered the hikers were not begging, they skirted past them and went their own ways.

The hikers were the forerunners of another tribe of fresh-air fiends who were discovering the joys of living a simple life in the open. The campers. They began to find their way up the farm road, laden with tents which they asked permission to pitch in the meadow or on any flat stretch of grass.

Jessie warned us, 'Ye'll a' be murdered in your beds. Ye'll need to lock your doors,' but we could never find the keys. And, to do them justice, the campers caused little trouble. Except that now and again they wanted to buy something, which was more of a nuisance to us than the tramps helping themselves from the henhouse or the garden.

'How much is milk?' I asked Mother one day when I had been approached by a camper with an empty jug and a ready purse. We had never bought or sold it before, so had no idea.

'Oh, just let them have it for nothing,' said Mother easily.

But as time went on we had such frequent requests to purchase eggs, butter, vegetables and scones, that Jessie grumbled, 'Dodsakes! ye'd think we were a shop. I'll need to set up a coonter in the kitchen.'

I would have liked that, for one of my earliest ambitions

had been to keep a sweet shop. The nearest I came to it was when Santa brought me a wonderful present one Christmas of a toy sweet shop complete with cardboard money, tiny scales and wee bottles of coloured sweets.

I played with it for ages and pestered Jessie and Jock-the-herd to be my customers. I remember the herd searching in his pocket for a coin and saying, 'Man-lassie, I'll hae a bawbees' worth o' pandrops to sook.'

My shop did not stock pandrops, so he had to make do with Dolly's Delights instead. They were bright pink and so highly scented that when he put one in his mouth and took the first suck, he spat it out. 'They'll puzzen me,' he complained. 'Pit them into the pigs' pail.'

Nothing poisoned Grumphy, who got all our leftovers and seemed to thrive on such a diet, but I was not going to waste Dolly's Delights on the sow, so I sucked them myself and survived.

It was the pig who caused most commotion to the campers, routing round their tents in search of sustenance, chewing at the ropes and knocking over the small stoves on which they brewed their tea. The cocks and hens, too, invaded their privacy, pecking at any crumb they could find, as if they had never been fed in their lives. But the campers did not complain. It was a price they were willing to pay for the novelty of living like gypsies.

One day I came a cropper over a tent rope and fell flat on my face. My face did not matter so much, it was the eggs I was carrying at the time. A whole basketful which it had taken me ages to collect from the obscure hiding places the perverse hens preferred to their own nests. Jessie, of course, called me a careless hussy, but Jock-the-herd was on my side.

'Thae folk canna pit up their tents for toffy!' he said, and hammered in the pegs so firmly that the campers had great difficulty getting them out when they moved on.

Another day I was surprised to find a camper – or was he

a hiker? – sitting sneezing in the kitchen wrapped in a
blanket with his feet in a tin basin of hot water, while Jessie
sat nearby with a grim expression on her face, mending a
large tear in the seat of his trousers.

'Tore it on the barbed-wire fence,' she informed me, 'an'
then went an' tummlet in the burn.' She said nothing more
in his hearing but plenty when he left, after being fortified
with a cup of tea and a dose of castor oil which she forced
him to swallow. 'It'll kill or cure him. I'm no' carin'
whuch.'

The comers and goers, as we called them, caused us some
problems with their fetish for cleanliness. The tramps made
their ablutions, if at all, in the horse trough or water barrel,
giving themselves a lick and a promise without benefit of
soap and towels, not bothering about such niceties as cleaning their teeth. If any. Not so their superior brethren.

'May I trouble you for a hot bath?' a wanderer once asked
at the front door. 'I'll pay for it.'

How much was a hot bath? The loan of a towel? A
bandage for a blistered heel? The hikers suffered more from
sore feet than the vagrants who were accustomed to tramp-
ing over rough ground. Many of them were limping by the
time they reached our door and had to remind themselves
they were doing it for pleasure. Others were so enamoured
with life on a farm that, after camping for a night, they were
reluctant to move on and asked if they could stay to help
with the hay making.

'Daft deevils!' Jock-the-herd called them; but the comers
and goers brought a bit of life to the place, with their strange
garbs: deerstalker hats, plus-fours, leather boots; and once a
lady in trousers!

'Nae leddy!' said Jessie. 'She needs a skelpit bottom,' and
we could see plenty of it as she scrambled over a dyke in her
tight breeks.

My most vivid memory of the comers and goers is of
that windy night when all the trees in the wood were

bowing and bending as if their backs would break. The storm had come on at the gloaming. The cocks and hens scuttered for shelter, slates came skiting off the roof, and we had to sneck all the doors and windows to keep them from rattling. Even so, the wind seemed to be inside the house as well as out.

Lying in bed, I could hear it roaring like an angry giant, buffeting the old farmhouse as if it would knock it down, dying away for a moment only to gather force for the next onslaught.

It was a pitch-black night, but through the window I could see strange flashes in the sky. Not lightning. Could it be that eerie thing called wildfire? I turned on my pillow, hid my head beneath the blankets and fell into a disturbed dream, from which I had a startling awakening, roused by the doorbell, not with one ring but with a continuous, urgent summons.

I was in the middle of the floor in my bare feet at the first jangle, and presently I heard Father in his carpet slippers slip-slopping down the stairs and the bell still ringing. We were all behind him in various stages of disarray by the time he opened the door and let the wind rush in.

We could see nothing, but above the scream of the storm we heard a woman's distraught voice. 'We've lost the baby! The baby's lost!'

Then a man's deeper voice. 'The tent's blown away and the baby with it.'

'The baby's lost!' shrieked the woman again. 'Blown away! Help us to find her.'

I had played with the baby before the storm started, when the couple arrived in a motorcycle and sidecar. She was a chubby child, only months old, warmly wrapped in woollen shawls, with nothing but her turned-up nose showing. I shoogled her in my arms while the man set up the tent and the woman lit their stove to make tea.

'Fancy travellin' aboot wi' a babby,' Jessie had said disapprovingly. But the tinks and tramps had no problems with *their* babbies, walking the roads with them securely anchored on their backs. I had left the campers' baby kicking up her heels on a rug in a corner of the tent while their parents took their tea.

And now she was lost. Blown away!

'Light the lantern,' called Father, taking command, while Mother drew the hysterical woman inside, trying to calm her with soothing words.

'It's all right. They'll find the baby. Come in out of the storm.'

Nothing would stop me from joining the search party. I found a pair of old boots, pulled on a mackintosh and went off after the men. The force of the gale blew me sideways, and I kept falling as I followed the lantern's light. There was no sign of the tent, no sign of the baby; but soon another light came flickering towards us, and when I bumped into Jock-the-herd, I felt our troubles were over.

'Man-lassie, what's up?'

When I told him he took it all in his stride, accustomed to looking for lost sheep. He gauged the way the wind was blowing, though this was difficult since it was swirling and changing direction, and set off purposefully with the rest of us tagging behind.

He found the tent first, tattered and torn behind a dyke; the baby next, after poking about with his crook in the ditch where she had lain sheltered from the fury of the storm, still wrapped in her shawls. Unharmed, thank goodness.

It was strange to be sitting in the lamplit kitchen in the wee sma' hoors, drinking tea and the men having a dram, with the baby back in her mother's arms, gooing as if nothing had happened. Mother had stirred the embers into life with kindling, and had a bright fire blazing. And, now the danger was past, we were all excitedly talking and laughing as if we were at a party.

There was a great sorting-out of beds before we all

settled down for the remainder of the night, by which time the storm had settled, too, and the cocks were crowing.

The man and woman kept in touch with us for years afterwards, sending us postcards from their travels and always signing them from the blown-away baby.

4. Happy Honeymoon

I remember the day – I must have been very young at the time – when I first heard the word 'honeymoon'. I liked the sound of it, though I had no notion what it was.

'What's a honeymoon, Jessie?'

'Hoots! a lot o' daft nonsense.'

That made it sound even better. Was I not full of daft nonsense myself?

'But what is't, Jessie?' I persisted. 'They're coming here for it.'

'Whae?'

'Him and her. Cousin Andrew and Jean Somebody.'

'He's no' your cousin. He's twice removed, an' she's Jean Armstrong. Silly things!'

What was silly about them, I wondered?

'There's mony a slip,' she said tartly. 'Onyway, they're no' mairret yet.'

But they soon would be.

There was a great to-do getting the spare room ready,

with the tykabed turned and the best pillow cases put on, the ones with the lace edges. The patchwork quilt was laid on top and finally the white crocheted coverlet. It looked a treat.

So did Father when he was toshed up in his cutaway suit – his tails – and lum hat. Every inch the fine gentleman, with a flower in his buttonhole and a gold pin in his tie. Mother made a good match for him in a delicate dovegrey dress with rows of little pearl buttons down the front, frills at her wrists, and a feathered toque on her head. She wore a long loose coat to disguise the fact that there would soon be another baby in the cradle.

After the wedding, Father and Mother were to bring the honeymoon couple back with them in the motor. I could hardly wait to see what they looked like. A fairytale prince and princess, I imagined.

The hours in between seemed endless, though Jessie, with her hands full in the kitchen, kept me and the Carthorse on the hop.

'Rin oot an' fetch some mint frae the gairden. I need it for the stuffin'. Mint, mind; no' weeds.'

'I ken the difference,' sniffed Liz-Ann, trailing away. Jessie never credited anyone with common sense, least of all the Carthorse.

'As for you.' She turned on me. 'Ye can help to set the table. Get oot the epergne.'

The epergne was a pest. Cleaning, polishing and assembling the different bits and pieces was a fikey job; but it looked nice when it was all set up and filled with flowers, with greenery trailing from the centrepiece to the little gates at the corners.

There was a great cleaning of cutlery. The best tureens, ashets and dinner plates were brought out, and starched napkins set at each place. Liz-Ann got her lugs boxed for breathing heavily on a pudding spoon before wiping it on her apron.

'Slaisterkites!' Jessie raged at her. I wished she would sometimes say a kind word to the Carthorse. It might have made all the difference.

I tried it myself.

'It'll be your turn next, Liz-Ann. You and George.'

Slaisterkites though she was, the Carthorse had a lad whom she addressed as Gorge when she had to pen a letter to him. A painful process. She always enlisted my help, and together we concocted stilted epistles to Gorge. Messages about meeting at the road-end on her day off. Signed, yours truly, Liz-Ann. Never with love. That would be going too far.

According to Jessie, George was not worth a docken, but romance comes in different guises, and he was the one bright spot in the Carthorse's drab life.

She blushed scarlet when I mentioned his name and said, 'Dinna be daft!' at the thought of her and George being next; but I knew she was pleased.

She contemplated the completed table and said, 'Terrible nice. But it needs a wee touch.'

'What kind of wee touch?'

'Mair like a waddin'.'

What would make it more like a wedding? We had no little marriage bells or orange blossom, but I suddenly bethought myself of something that would add a touch of brightness. The red rowanberries were ripe in the wood.

I sped away and gathered some colourful clusters. Liz-Ann helped me to strip off the berries, and we formed them into scarlet hearts on the white tablecloth wherever we could find empty spaces between cruets and cutlery. Some of the hearts were a little lopsided but the effect was cheerful.

'The Lord kens what Jessie'll say,' remarked the Carthorse, as we stood back to admire our handiwork.

She said plenty, but things were reaching boiling point in the kitchen, so though she gave us the roughest edge of her tongue she left the table alone. With the lamps lit and the fires burning brightly, the house looked warm and welcoming.

'This is them!' cried Liz-Ann, having spied the car lights from the window. 'We'll need to chuck something at them.'

'What'll we chuck?' I queried.

'Rice,' said the Carthorse, rushing to the kitchen press.

Jessie protested at the waste of good rice and at the mess we would make, but at the last moment she got carried away herself and grabbed a handful from the jar. When the happy couple came in through the front door we lurked in the shadows of the dimly lit lobby and hurled the rice at them.

They laughed as they ducked the bombardment. Father and Mother, too, looked merry, and even Jessie conjured up a smile as she shook hands with the newly-weds. The bride was rosy-cheeked and the groom well scrubbed, though a trifle uncomfortable in his good suit. Very relieved when Father said, 'Take off your jacket, Andrew man.'

The merriment continued throughout the meal, even when Liz-Ann dropped a dish of brussels sprouts. The rowan hearts got scattered all over the table but not before everyone had admired them. I watched the bride twisting the new wedding ring on her finger and the groom putting a possessive hand over hers. No wonder the Carthorse gave a sentimental sigh as she swept up the sprouts from the floor.

Before my head began to nod I remember Father getting to his feet with a glass in his hand to make a speech, which ended with funny stories which I had heard many times before, but which never failed to make me kink with laughter. Then it all became a blur till Jessie hauled me out of the room and said firmly, 'Awa' up the stair to your bed.'

Looking back, I realize what a nuisance I must have been to cousin Andrew and his bride. The honeymoon lasted a week and the couple were quite content to be left alone; but I kept following them around on their solitary walks and suggesting little treats in case they were fed up.

'Would you like a wee game of hide-and-seek?'

'No, not just now.'

'What about coming up the hill to see my castle?'

'No thanks, we're going the other way.'

Sometimes by special dispensation from the Boss they took refuge in the greenhouse where they sat side by side amongst the sprouting seedboxes. I never actually saw them kissing, but they often held hands, and the bride would say, 'Oh, Andrew!' in response to the groom's 'Oh, Jean!'

It was a strange thing, a honeymoon.

The beasts did not bother with weddings or the minister's blessing. They just got on with it. I was well aware of the end result. Following the visit of the stallion, there would be foals in the stable; and the bull was not kept on the farm merely for his beauty. I knew all about rams and lambing time, and about the cats kittling. They seemed to be doing that all the time.

Blackie, the kitchen cat, shed her load in peculiar places. In the boot cupboard, under the kitchen sink, or the parlour sofa; once even in the middle of the spare bed.

'She's at it again,' Jessie would sniff, seeing the cat searching around for a hiding place. 'Nae doot aboot it, we'll need to get rid o' this lot.'

It was a threat she used every time Blackie produced a new brood. 'Pit them in a poke an' droon them in the waitter barrel.' I fought tooth and nail against this fearful fate. Usually, after falling over them as they crawled about the kitchen, we set them free to run about the farm, or tried to find good homes for them. Not an easy job, since country folk were over-supplied with kittens already.

So what about townfolk?

I remember spreading the news in my class at the Gram-

mar School when Blackie was due for another family.
There was only one taker. Lucy, the Ewe-Lamb, wanted a
kitten.

'A wee black one with white paws,' she specified. 'I'm
going to call her Cinderella.'

'But it might be male.'

'I don't care. I'll call it Cinderella. When will it be born?'

She deived me about it every day till I was forced to say to
Blackie, 'Hurry up,' but the cat took her own time. Never
had she been so slow in searching out a suitable haven. I
tried to encourage her by finding an old clothes basket,
lining it with rags and placing it in a secluded corner of the
lobby. Time and again I took Blackie there and introduced
her to her couch, but she just turned her back and stalked
away with her nose in the air. In the end she did the deed in
an inaccessible spot behind the piano. One tortyshell, one
blue-grey, one snow-white, one streaked like a tiger. Not
one that looked like the Ewe-Lamb's idea of Cinderella.

When I told Lucy about them she asked excitedly if she
could come out to the farm and choose for herself. 'No,' I
said firmly, recalling her previous visit which had not been
a success. I described them to her instead, as best I could.
She changed her mind every day and finally decided on the
tiger kitten. 'But I'm still going to call her Cinderella. When
will you bring her in? I can't wait.'

'You'll have to. Her eyes aren't open yet and her
mother's feeding her.'

'Oh, but I could feed her better. I'll get her liver and
cream and the best fish. I've got a nice basket for her
already, and a fluffy ball to play with, and a wee toy mouse.'

I began to feel sorry for Cinderella faced with such a
pampered future. She would easily survive the rough life on
the farm, but how would she put up with all the smothering
that awaited her?

'I'm dying to see her. *When* will you bring her?'

The day came. My problem was how to convey Cinderella to Jedburgh. In my schoolbag alongside the dreaded Latin lesson-book? No! It seemed she disliked it as much as I did, for she was no sooner in than she was out. In the end, after a sad parting from Blackie, she snuggled into my arms, and I carried her down the road to wait at Mary-Ann's for the school bus.

'Hullo, cheetie-pussy,' she said to the kitten.

Mary-Anne was feeding her hens from her apron pocket. If Cinderella had been a chicken, the old woman would have taken more notice of her. As it was, she threw a handful of corn to Jock Tamson, the cockerel, and remarked fondly, 'A terrible appetite Jock's got. Still, he pits it in a guid skin.'

Mary-Anne had names for all her flock and talked to them as if they were human beings. She spared a moment to look at the kitten. 'I've heard o' Mary had a little lamb, but fancy a cat gaun to the schule! Here's the bus. Ta-ta, lassie.'

It was a blessing Black Sandy, the driver, was so easy-osy, or he would have pitched Cinderella overboard. With the movement of the bus the kitten had turned frisky. Try as I would to restrain her, there was no keeping her still. She leapt from my arms, crawled under the seats, scratched at Black Sandy's trouser legs, and tried to climb on to his knee.

'Stop scartin' ma legs, ye wee rascal.'

But nothing would stop Cinderella, and her antics did not stop Big Sandy from bawling out his songs.

' "My bonnie lies over the ocean. . . ." Ca' canny, ye wee deevil. "My bonnie lies over the sea. . . ." '

What a relief when we reached Jedburgh and found Lucy waiting for the handover at the school gate. Her mother was with her, as planned, ready to convey Cinderella to her new home in a little basket, all prettily lined, like a layette.

The Ewe-Lamb was dancing with impatience. 'Where is she? I want to hold her. Let me see!'

The kitten was under the back seat. I had to crawl up and down the dusty bus before I finally retrieved her.

'Here!' I said, thankfully handing her over to Lucy. That would be the end of Cinderella as far as I was concerned.

Not a bit of it.

Lucy hugged the kitten tightly, too tightly, and went into ecstasies. 'Oh! isn't she nice! Nice wee Cinderella. Good wee pussy cat. Let me give you a kiss and a cuddle.' A shriek from the Ewe-Lamb. 'Oh! she's scratching my face. Bad Cinderella!'

Having left her mark on her new mistress's face, bad Cinderella leapt from her arms and sat down in the gutter. I lifted her into the layette, but she would have none of it. Once more she took a leap and landed back in the gutter. At which point the school bell rang. It sounded like a death knell.

'What'll we do?' wailed the Ewe-Lamb, nursing her scratched cheek. 'Cinderella, be a good wee pussy cat,' she said desperately. 'Go home in the basket with mum and you'll get a nice juicy piece of liver. Then you can play with your toy mouse till I come home at lunchtime. . . .'

She was wasting her breath. No blandishments had any effect on the kitten, who continued to sit as still as a stooky, while the janny advanced on us ready to slam the school gate against all latecomers. We had to go in or be marked absent, leaving Lucy's distraught mother outside, holding the empty basket.

At the last moment, Cinderella suddenly came to life and decided to follow us, darting through the janny's legs and wandering away up towards the classrooms. I ran after her in a panic and snatched her up at the school door.

'Come on, you! Behave yourself,' I said sternly. 'You're a perfect pest.' Cinderella gave an unrepentant miaow and snuggled contentedly in my arms, purring away like a kettle on the boil.

'Oh d-dear! where can we hide her till lunchtime?' asked Lucy breathlessly, running after me. It was a question I could not answer.

The simplest solution seemed to be to smuggle her into the classroom and hope for the best. I knew we were dicing with death, especially as it was Mary-Ann Crichton's class, and that she had once told us she was allergic to cats. I was not sure what allergic meant, but I knew Miss Crichton did not like cats, or any other creatures. She did not like us much either.

Luckily the kitten went to sleep on my knee and for a time I forgot about her. What I recall most vividly about that morning is watching a fat furry bumblebee crawling up the windowpane.

I followed its progress closely instead of listening to Miss Crichton, marvelling at the mastermind who had created all such creatures. For what purpose? I pondered about the bumblebee's private life. Where was its mother? Perhaps it was a prodigal son and she was out searching for him in a distraught state. Surely it would prefer the freedom of the open air to imprisonment in a stuffy classroom.

Suddenly the bumblebee took off and went winging away over the blackboard. Then it zoomed around Mary-Ann Crichton's head as if searching for a suitable landing place.

Miss Crichton let out a scream, grabbed the chalk duster, and began flapping it at the bumblebee.

'Get that beast out! Quick!'

There was an uproar while the big boys, delighted to abandon their lessons, sprang into action and rampaged around the classroom as if chasing a wild boar. I was afraid they might succeed in exterminating their prey but, after a great to-do about opening wide the window, the bumblebee finally flew off to freedom.

'Good for you!' I said under my breath. 'Away home to your mammy.'

Miss Crichton had a hard job settling the class down after such excitement, and was nippier than usual when she resumed the lesson. I ducked my head, hoping not to be noticed, while the kitten on my lap continued to purr contentedly. Lucky thing! *She* did not have to bother her head about French verbs.

I did.

'*Dormir,*' rapped Mary-Ann, aiming her pointer at me. 'What do you know about the verb?'

Not much.

'*Je dors,*' I began feebly and then stuck.

'Stupid girl! Up on your feet.'

There was little sleeping for me when I obeyed her instruction and stood up, suddenly decanting Cinderella on to the floor. The kitten let out an indignant *miaow* and scuttled across the classroom, making a dead set at Miss Crichton.

'Help!' she screamed, as if she had been charged by a tiger. 'Get that beast out! Quick!'

It was not Miss Crichton's day. Nor mine.

'Who let that beast in?' she demanded from behind the blackboard, as I rushed after Cinderella and caught her up in my arms. 'You! I might have known. How dare you! Wicked girl! You'll be punished. I'll see to that!'

'I'm s-sorry, Miss Crichton. You see. . . .'

Miss Crichton did not see. 'Out! Take it out! Get rid of that beast at once. Give it to the janitor. Wicked girl! You'll be punished!'

The Ewe-Lamb sat through the whole episode with reddening cheeks, scratch and all, and did not utter a word in my defence. Not that I expected it of her.

The janny did not jump for joy when I sought him out and asked if he would look after the kitten till lunchtime. Especially since I disturbed him having a quiet smoke in the nether regions, known as hell, sitting on a heap of coke reading the *Squeaker*.

'Bloomin' pest!' I was not sure whether he was referring to me or the kitten. 'I've a guid mind to fling the baith o' ye into the boiler.'

In the end he shut Cinderella in a cupboard, but not, I was pleased to see, before she had left her mark on his bare arm. My responsibilities for the kitten were now over, though for a time I had to listen to daily bulletins from Lucy who extolled Cinderella's virtues like a besotted parent.

The poor kitten's spirit must have been cowed, and doubtless she grew lethargic on rich living, for there were no more scratches to be seen on her mistress's cheeks.

'Of course,' said Lucy complacently, 'it must make such a difference to her living with us. She's got everything she wants. You should see how fat she is. She can hardly move.'

Poor Cinderella.

I got my punishment, of course. Dozens of verbs, irregular and otherwise. And for ages Miss Crichton referred to me as 'that beastly girl'.

But better things were on their way. For at last I found someone to love. Nicer than a kitten.

A human being.

5. The Dumpling

It was one of those sparkling days when the sun was shining high in the sky like a bright arc light, yet with a tingle in the air, enough to freshen the face, clear the head, and cause the blood to course. A day for activity outside, not for lounging in the house.

Saturday, a day of freedom.

I ran out through the kitchen door and swallowed the air, gulping it down like good wine. It went to my head, making me feel light-hearted enough to jump for the joy of living. I began to sing. Anything to give vent to my high spirits.

> 'Come fill up my cup, come fill up my can,
> Come saddle the horses, and call out the men;
> Come open the gates and let me gang free,
> For it's up wi' the bonnets o' Bonnie Dundee.'

A skylark was singing a sweeter song overhead. The hills stood out stark and clear. Big Cheviot, the Eildons, our own hill where my ruined castle stood. The whole farm was like a tangled garden. Wild roses, foxgloves, clover, vetch, violets, all growing where they pleased. Their combined perfume was heady, mingled though it was with the more pungent aroma of newly spread dung.

Remember this in years to come, I told myself. A moment to capture. As if I could put it in my pocket, or press it between the pages of a book. But I *have* kept it. It is with me now. I can turn the clock back and sniff the fragrance of crab-apple blossom, hear the call of the curlew, and another sound. The sound of Jock-the-herd's voice.

It was coming from the work stable. What was Jock doing there? I went round to see. When I heard the clash of his shears I knew. He was clipping the hinds' hair, an operation worth watching.

When their rough locks grew too straggly the men persuaded the herd to act as barber. He treated them much as he did the sheep. Snip-snap! Take it or leave it.

'Mind ma lug!' they would protest, for there was often a spot or two of blood to be seen before the deed was done.

'Hoots! haud your wheesht!' the herd would say. 'I'll dab on a bit ointment.' Ointment being the black sticky mess he kept in a round tin box for the purpose of soothing the sheep's wounds. A balm for all ailments from ringworm to loupin' ill.

No need for Jock to be shorn himself. He hid his baldness under his bonnet and only displayed his bare powe in the kirk where I found it fascinating to watch the steam rising from the top of his cranium, like a kettle on the boil.

Father went to a real barber in Jedburgh, with a striped pole outside and unknown mysteries within. I was topped and tailed at home by Jessie, who singed the ends of my hair before giving it a vigorous going-over with a small tooth-comb, to take out the rugs and make sure I hadn't caught 'beasts'.

I never saw the hinds combing their own hair, though

they kept a large comb – the currycomb, it was called – for use on the Clydesdales. They took more pride in attending to *their* manes than their own; but now and again in desperation they were forced to get their tousled thatches fleeced.

When I entered the stable, Wull was sitting on a wooden stool, submitting to the herd's ministrations. Tam had already been cropped. He looked younger and somehow more vulnerable as he thrust his rough hands through the hair that was left. 'By jings! ye've gied it a gliff this time, Jock,' he protested. 'I'd better pit on ma bunnett or I'll catch ma daith o' cauld.'

'Sit still, you!' the herd was telling his next customer. 'Dod! ye're mair fashious than a yowe.'

He had caught Wull in a vice-like grip round the neck to stop him from squirming, and was snipping away in a slapdash fashion, with clumps of hair cascading on to the stable floor. I liked to listen to them catter-battering. It was a strange form of dialogue.

Suddenly I heard another sound. The motor backfiring.

Tam cocked his ears. 'That's the Boss awa' on the randan. Daursay, whaur's he aff to the day?'

For the men liked to keep track of the Boss's comings and goings; and the Boss, never secretive about his movements, often came round to put them in the picture. Sometimes his jaunts took him to Swinside Townhead, his other farm in the Oxnam district, or to Jedburgh to sit on a committee. A strange performance, I thought.

'The Boss canna say no,' sniffed Jessie.

So Father said yes, and off he went on any ploy that would take him into company. I liked to hear his stories when he came back, for he always had some comical incident to relate.

'I'd sooner bide at hame an' hear the Boss tell aboot it than gang on a jaunt masel',' the men often said. Though sometimes they went to Jedburgh themselves on a Saturday night, cycling there and back, but what they did when they reached the town remained a mystery to me. Did they go to the pictures, or have a dram in the Carters' Rest? Or just stand about in the marketplace? They were always dour the next day, and, unlike the Boss, had no funny tales to tell. A strange mixture they were. Secretive about themselves, and yet they liked to hear all the doorstep gossip.

'He's never let dab,' Wull said in an aggrieved voice, as Tin Lizzie went rattling away into the distance.

'Haud still!' The herd snipped off the last tuft. 'Likely he's gane to the rugby.'

Then I remembered, and my high spirits took a downward plunge.

'He's away to fetch the nurse from the train.'

The nurse! Little wonder a black cloud descended on me at the thought of that prim starched figure who would rule the roost in the weeks to come.

'Thon madam!' Jessie called her. 'Aye wantin' wee trays. An', "Are you sure the jug's clean?" Set her up!'

There was a strained atmosphere in the house from the moment she set foot in it.

The nurse came from Kelso, and Father was away in to Jedburgh to collect her and her neat luggage from the station. She always installed herself well in advance of the baby's arrival, and stayed for a week or two until Mother was set on her feet. Father, I knew, would spend more time in the greenhouse to keep out of her way, but there was no avoiding the stress of mealtimes when she presided in place of Mother. And woe betide Jessie if there was a stain on the tablecloth. Her sharp eyes spotlighted all our flaws.

Especially mine. She had an oblique way of pointing them out. 'Don't you think it would be nicer if you straightened your stockings? Tied back your hair? Closed the door gently? Mended that tear in your jersey? Finished up the cabbage on your plate? Tiptoed up the stairs?' Her, and her eternal 'Hushes'!

I did not dislike her. Wicked or not, I hated her.

Mother was the only one who got on with her. I think she enjoyed the nurse's attention; being told to put her feet up, having hot milk and wee biscuits to eat, listening to tales about other babies the nurse had brought into the world. A lord once, no less.

'Is it to be a laddie or a lassie this time?' Tam was asking.

I did not care. I only knew the wooden cradle would soon be brought down from the garret, and it would start all over again. The mysterious whisperings, the doctor's arrival, the feeble squalling of the new baby, the tiptoeing upstairs to keek round the bedroom door – nurse permitting – the sight of mother with a pleased look on her face reclining on her pillows, wearing a pink bedjacket and cradling a bundle in her arms.

The other baby, the one next to me, was only just toddling around, pulling things off the table and girning if he didn't get his own way. I looked after him if I had to, but as yet he had no personality, and we were not attuned in any way. Maybe a wee girl would be nice for a change. Maybe not.

'Man-lassie! ye've fairly got your nose oot o' joint noo,' said the herd, putting away his shears.

But when had my nose not been out of joint?

The dark cloud grew blacker till it almost swamped me with despair. Then Tam, not usually given to profound statements, remarked, 'We're a' in the hands o' providence.'

'Ay,' agreed Wull, as if he had just heard a great truth. 'We micht as weel mak' the best o' things.'

So I decided I would. I would make the best of this sparkling day before the nurse's arrival blotted out the sun. Begone dull care. Off I ran to my refuge on the hill, splashing barefoot through the burn in the wood, disturbing the cushy-doos in the trees, climbing up the crumbling castle walls and settling down contentedly to gaze at my favourite scene.

'O what hills are yon, yon pleasant hills,
That the sun shines sweetly on?'
'O yon are the hills of heaven,' he said,
'Where you will never won.'

The earthly hills were good enough for me, and surely heaven was here. In the distance I could see the winding main road, and if I narrowed my eyes I could make out the minister wheeling his bicycle in through the manse gate. Was that the baker and his horse? I sat drowsing in the sun, trying to picture the hillside in bygone days when reivers crept through the bracken and the peace was shattered with the clash of steel.

My own peace came to an end when I heard through my reveries the tinny tinkle of the dinner bell which Jessie rang to summons me home. I did not want to give up a moment of this fine free day, so I turned a deaf ear.

Ding-dong-ding!

There it was again. Usually Jessie gave up after the first few rings. Not today. There was something different about the sound of the bell. An urgency, as if the call must be obeyed. Perhaps I had better go.

Reluctantly, I scrambled down from my perch, dislodging some more of the old stones. I realized sadly that my castle was becoming smaller and that I was helping it to dwindle. Maybe I could build it up again, stone upon stone, as the herd painstakingly built his dykes.

Ding-dong-ding!

What was Jessie up to? Who cared if her stovies were over-cooked? I had missed dozens of meals in my time, so why was she bothering today?

As I started to run home, I realized the sound of the bell was growing louder, as if Jessie was coming to meet me. Yes! there she was, making her way up the loaning that led to the hill, waving and beckoning on me to hurry. Something was up.

'Hurry, lassie,' she called breathlessly. 'Ye'll need to rin.'

'Run! Where? What's wrong?'

'It's the mistress. She's started. An' the creddle no' even doon.'

And the nurse not here! 'Mercy!' I gasped. 'Have you rung for the doctor?'

'That's it. The tellyphone's no' workin'. It's deid. Canna get a word oot o't.'

For once Jessie looked at the end of her tether.

'So what'll we do?' I asked, feeling my pulse beating faster with apprehension.

'Ye'll need to rin doon to Camptoon to Bella at the post office. Get her to ring for the doctor.'

'Yes, I will,' I said, getting ready to sprint. 'Is Mother very ill?'

'Just the usual,' said Jessie, hurrying back to the house. 'Rin, lassie, rin.'

I ran like the wind. It was a blessing it was all downhill. A mile and a bit. Past the cottages, past the big hedges, down the bumpy road, over the steep brae. A stitch in my side, never mind that. Past the smiddy, up the road to Mary-Anne's. Camptown! Hurry into Bella's shop.

'Losh, lassie! what's up?'

I hung over the counter, hardly able to speak.

'Mother! Get the doctor! Our telephone's broken down.'

And then the miracle happened.

'The doctor!' cried Bella, rising to the emergency. 'My! ye're in luck, lassie. He's next door lookin' at auld Mrs Eliot's leg. Did ye no' see his car ootside?'

No! I had been too busy running to notice anything. But there it was, with the chauffeur sitting at the wheel. And by the time I dashed out of the shop the doctor himself was emerging from old Mrs Eliot's door.

I stammered out my story, forgetting my fear of the great man who was looking at me coldly over his pince-nez, as if wondering who I was, though he had brought *me* into the world, too, in the far distant past. But he got the gist of what I was trying to say, and seemed suddenly to recognize me.

'Overton Bush! Right!' he said briskly. 'I'll go straight there now. Do you want a lift home?'

I shook my head. I had done my job, but I could not face the prospect of sitting in the back of the car beside the great doctor. I walked home slowly, taking my time up the steep brae. Everything would be all right now.

I was nearing home when I heard the sound of the rattletrap behind me, a very different equipage from the doctor's. Father was at the wheel with a set expression on his face, and the nurse sitting bolt upright beside him, her gloved hands in her lap. I could sense her disapproval when she saw me. What a ticket! Bare legs, dishevelled hair, and a disconnected story to shout through the window as the car slowed down.

'It's all right. The doctor's there,' I ended as Father's face flushed with alarm and the nurse looked thoroughly put out. The car shot past me, putting on a spurt on the last lap home, and I continued on my solitary way. But I felt I had done something to justify my existence.

When I got into the kitchen I saw that a tray had been set out for the doctor, or maybe for Mother or the nurse, with a lace-edged cloth and the best china. Jessie was sitting at the table – unusual for her – leaning on her elbows and sipping tea from a plain cup. She looked drained, as if she had been through goodness-knew-what.

'Is . . . is everything all right, Jessie?'

She nodded and took another sip of tea. 'The babby's here. A laddie.'

'Oh, that's fine.'

Laddie or lassie, I did not care as long as things were all right.

Jessie set down her cup and said with a touch of complacency, 'An' we managed withoot thon madam.'

'Oh, well done, Jessie!'

I felt like shaking hands with her, as if we had done it together. Then I asked, 'What's he like, Jessie? The baby?'

'A wee dumpling,' said Jessie, and there was a faint smile on her tired face as she spoke.

So that was what we called him. The Dumpling.

Jessie was an adept at making dumplings. Specially clooty dumplings. She was a hitty-missy kind of cook, never bothering about recipes.

'I keep them in ma heid,' she declared and, when asked what ingredients she used, would say, 'A wee tait o' this, an' a wee tait o' that.' (A 'tait' was a small quantity.) 'A nieve-fou o' this, an' a nieve-fou o' that.' (A 'nieve-fou' was a handful.) 'Rummle them a' thegither, an' that's it.' Measuring to an exact specification was not for Jessie.

Her clooty dumplings always turned out a treat. Boiled in a cloth (a 'cloot'), packed full of currants, sultanas, spices – 'a wee tait o' this, an' a wee tait o' that' – depending on the contents of the kitchen cupboard at the time, Jessie's dumplings had a rich, satisfying flavour, after bubbling for hours in a big pan at the side of the fire. The great moment came when it was lifted out and the cloot unwrapped to reveal the appetizing contents within.

'No' bad,' Jessie would say, trying to conceal her satisfaction at the sight of the masterpiece she had created.

But now she had helped to produce the best dumpling of all.

He was everybody's baby from the start, smiling at anyone, even the sour-faced nurse. She, of course, did her best to keep me at a distance. 'No, no! *You*'re far too clumsy to hold him.' So I had to bide my time till the happy day when Father, trying not to look too pleased, drove 'thon madam' back into town to catch the train to Kelso.

'That'll be the lot!' he said when he came back.

But he was wrong. There was one more to come.

Meanwhile the Dumpling laughed his way into

everyone's heart. Even Jessie shoogled him in her arms and sang ditties to him, as she patted his back to get the wind up.

> 'Deedle-deedle-dumpling,
> My son John
> Went to bed
> With his britches on.'

He cooed and gurgled, he blew frothy bubbles, and seemed delighted to be alive. Obviously he had inherited Father's funnybone, for he often chuckled to himself as if recalling a private joke. What a pity, I thought, that babies could not master the language as soon as they were born. By the time they learnt to speak they had forgotten all the fascinating things they might have told us.

When the Dumpling began to crawl, he talked gibberish to Blackie the cat, who appeared to understand every word he said. I longed for an interpreter.

At that time he was the one bright spot in my life. Lavish as he was with his favours, I imagined he had a special smile for me. I carried him about till my arms ached, and hurried home from school for the pleasure of seeing him clapping his hands at my approach. He could not say, 'Hullo! How did you get on today?' but I felt that was in his mind. So I told him. I confided all sorts of things to the Dumpling, who beamed back at me, pulled my nose, and sometimes uttered unintelligible sounds, as if I was Blackie the cat.

It was a new experience for me, this fond feeling for someone. In the midst of all my vicissitudes, I consoled myself with the thought, 'Never mind; there's always the Dumpling.'

6. Swings and Roundabouts

'What about it?' Father would say, and we knew his itchy feet were tickling him.

He was a great one for springing surprises on the spur of the moment. I think he sometimes surprised himself. Having got up in the morning with no intention of going anywhere, he would suddenly yoke Flora the pony into the gig, or reverse Tin Lizzie out of the garage. Then it was up and away.

Luckily, Mother was of the same temperament. If the baby was asleep in the cradle and Jessie in charge of the household, she would willingly take off her apron, tie on her motoring veil, and say, 'That's me ready.'

It might only be a run over to the other farm, at Swinside, a visit to a roup, or a jaunt into Jedburgh. But it was an outing, a break in the monotony, a chance to see other faces; a better tonic than the doctor's medicine. And sometimes Father had an ace up his sleeve and a secret look on his face.

'No, I'm not telling you,' he would say, as we jogged or rattled down the bumpy road. 'Wait and see.'

I remember the Saturday when I was included in one of these mysterious expeditions. Jessie saw us off at the door with the Dumpling in her arms. I would fain have stayed behind and taken charge of him myself, except for the surge of excitement I felt at the prospect of venturing into the unknown. Father was not the only one in the family with itchy feet.

Jessie expected us back before we ever got anywhere, which frequently was the case if the motor was in one of its moods. 'Ta-ta! I'll keep the kettle on the boil.'

She waved the baby's hand. No tears. The Dumpling laughed at the sound of Tin Lizzie backfiring. A sudden jolt forward and away we went down the road, with Father swerving to avoid the ruts. Safely past the cottages and as far as the road-end without mishaps. This was the exciting moment. In which direction would Father turn the wheel?

Left! And left again at Mary-Anne's, past Camptown and away up the road towards Edgerston. Past the village school. Auld Baldy-Heid was leaning over the garden gate. There was not much for him to do in the garden except lean, since he contrived to get his weeding done by the big boys as part of a lesson. Though I was now out of his clutches, I still shivered at the sight of him, remembering past punishments; but he only gave a casual wave as we rumbled by.

By now I realized we were in a for a real treat. A trip over the Carter Bar into England. It was a steep winding road towards the summit. Father shoogled in his seat as if urging the old horse onwards and upwards. We stopped at the frontier and I stood with one foot in each country, looking back at the land we had left.

'Come on! We'll be late,' called Father.

For what?

When we drove past Redeswire, past the Catcleuch

Reservoir, and neared the little village of Rothbury, I knew. The crowds were already gathering for the show, flocking from all parts of Cumberland and Northumberland, as well as some from our side of the Border. A busload, indeed, from Jedburgh. They had come, not only for the outing, to examine the flowers, vegetables and baking displays in the tents, but more particularly to watch the wrestlers.

We joined the group gathered in a circle to gape at the contestants. Stout fellows, stripped to their combinations and stocking soles, with great muscles rippling on their bare arms. The first pair were advancing to meet face to face in the centre of the ring. For a time they danced cautiously around, sizing each other up, then suddenly they got to grips, locking their hands behind their opponent's back, and the fight was on. More dancing and prancing, then a stockinged foot shot out as the one tried to trip the other off balance.

Meantime their supporters were shouting encouragement in the local twang.

'Watch out, hinny! Hang on, me lad! By! you've got him, Geordie!'

They continued to rock and wrestle till one lost his balance and fell down with a mighty thud. Then the victor helped the other up and shook hands. And it began all over again with another pair. There was a great deal of art and skill in it which I did not understand, but I liked watching the big men and listening to the comments of the crowd.

Presently everyone moved off to watch the hound trail, a special feature of the show. We had already seen the runner setting off amidst cheers to lay the trail, with a rag dipped in a strong solution of aniseed in his hand. Off he sped, trailing the rag on the ground, away up the hillside and disappeared from sight. Then back he came by a roundabout route, and all was ready for the race.

The hounds were lined up, tugging to be off, but firmly held back by their owners till the signal was given to set them free. A great shout went up when they were let loose. Some ran straight on the trail. Others strayed from side to side, losing the scent, while their distracted owners shouted at them from a distance. It was eerie hearing the hounds baying and howling, as if they were after blood.

When they vanished over the ridge we all relaxed, except the owners, who waited anxiously to see which dog would be the first to reappear. They held spyglasses to their eyes, scanning the horizon for a sight of a familiar nose or tail.

Then the shouting began and grew to a crescendo. The first dog had been sighted. Was it Ringer or Rattler or Dodger or Spring? The men worked themselves into a frenzy as they urged their hounds home, which was catching to the crowd, even if we did not know one animal from another.

We went inside one of the tents, heavy with the heady perfume of flowers. Father made straight for the sweetpeas – his speciality – and examined them from every angle. The ones he nurtured at home were just as good. Better, I thought; and Mother's sponge cakes might have won a prize ticket, if she had been showing. But the sight and smell of the home baking made us hungry, and we set off to look for sustenance.

A fat man at a stall was selling pies and lemonade. It was difficult to drink out of the bottle, for there was a wee round marble in the neck, which acted as a stopper. I had to shoogle it about to get a good gulp.

Meantime there was plenty to watch. The pillow fighters, perched on a high bar, thwacking at each other till they both lost balance and tumbled to the ground. The tug-of-war, with some of the stout wrestlers taking part and the rope creaking till it seemed it must break in the middle. The slow bicycle race, when the last man won, and the competitors had to keep going with the least movement possible, till they were forced to give in, fall off, or shoot past their opponents and lose the race.

On the way home I was so bemused by it all that I did not notice the motor hiccupping on the hills.

'Blast!' said Father as Tin Lizzie spluttered to a standstill. We all got out and helped to push her to the side. We were used to it, so we took it in our stride. A charabanc swerved past us without stopping, while Father opened the bonnet and peered helplessly inside.

'What the dickens is up with her now?' he said, scratching his head.

Usually it was water, or the lack of it, and I was sent to the nearest habitation to beg for help. It was all part of the regular routine of an outing. I preferred the pony and gig. Flora never went on strike.

Presently we heard a cheerful toot and a battered van drew in behind us. Out stepped the fat man who had been selling pies and lemonade at the show.

'Let's have a look,' said he, rolling up his sleeves.

Father gave a sigh of relief and thankfully let him get on with it, while we stood around spectating.

'Try her now,' said the lemonade man, wiping his hands on an oily rag. 'Crank her up.'

Father inserted the starting handle and swung it round. At last a welcome puttering sound was heard as Lizzie shuddered back to life.

'That's it!' said the man, returning to his van. 'Away you go!'

'Wait!' said Father, thrusting his hand into his pocket, but our rescuer would take no recompense. Not only that, he handed me another bottle of lemonade with a wee marble in the neck.

'There are some nice folk in the world,' said Mother as we set off once more on the homeward journey.

Then came the day when I read an announcement in the Jedburgh gazette – the *Squeaker*. The newspaper was spread on the kitchen table with the jelly pan on top of it. Red splatches of rowan jelly had spilled over on to the pages like blood, and Jessie was waiting for the contents to cool before filling the jam jars. I had already done my job by writing out 'ROWAN JELLY' on the little labels, as well as tasting the sample Jessie had poured into a saucer. It had a tart taste and would be used later on as an accompaniment for pheasant or hare. Looking back, it seemed we lived high, but our fare was all free and available on the farm. I thought sausages from the butcher the greatest treat.

'It's ready noo. Oot ma road,' said Jessie, seizing the ladle and stirring the contents of the pan.

'Wait, Jessie, wait!' I was craning my neck to read the announcement.

> A travelling fair is coming to Jedburgh.
> Hobby-horses. Coconut-shies. Lucky-dips.
> Aunt Sally. Fortune-tellers. Menagerie.
> Not to be missed!

'What's a menagerie, Jessie?'
'Never heard o't. Haud that jam jar steedy.'
'But what d'you think it might be, Jessie?'
'Hoots! it micht be onything. I'm no' a dictionary.'
But she had given me an idea, so when the rowan jelly was safely potted, I went and looked up the dictionary.

Menagerie. A collection of caged wild beasts taken round the country for exhibition.

I was not keen on caging beasts, but I was keen enough to go to the fair. This was something new and different. Not to be missed.

The next day I saw from the school bus as we were passing the Glebe on the outskirts of Jedburgh that the travelling people had arrived with their caravans, and were setting up stalls, erecting tents and assembling the round-abouts. I had an exciting glimpse of painted hobby-horses, of dark-skinned children darting about the field, of women dressed in vivid colours, sitting on the steps of their cara-vans, shaking out rugs, and cleaning the windows of their movable homes.

It was like a transformation scene, which faded from the eyes when Big Sandy revved up the bus and drove towards the staid High Street. But the sight was enough to stir the imagination and convince me that the fair was not to be missed. If Father could be persuaded to go. No difficulty about *that*! He would not have missed it himself.

Father gave me some spending money, and I wandered off on my own, taking my time to absorb all the sights and sounds of this strange new world, wondering what it would be like to lead a roving life with no roots, always in an uproar of shouting, music, clamour and unreality. Like living in a pantomime. How would one know when the curtain came down and real life began?

I stared long enough at the hobby-horses before gather-ing enough courage to step on to the wooden platform when they slowed down and climb astride one of the painted ponies. What would Flora have thought of this strange creature? Scarlet body, green saddle, blue reins and a bright yellow tail. I held tightly to its mane when the music started and we began to move round and round. Slowly at first. Oh! this was nice! I could even wave to one of my schoolfriends in the distance, but not when the music grew louder and the horses gathered speed, running an erratic race. Up one minute, down the next, galloping round in a mad chase, but never catching up on each other. My stomach went up and down, too. Hold tight!

The sky, the Glebe, the caravans, the tents, the people, all were whirling with me like drunken dervishes. Hang on! It would be terrible to tumble off in full view of everyone. Was that Mother looking anxiously at me? No! It was

Mother all right, but why should she look anxious? For now I had got the hang of it and could have floated round for ever. Let the music blare louder, the ponies jump higher. I felt like a bird soaring in the sky.

Too soon the ponies slowed down and I had to get off to let others take my place, but I went back again and again as long as my money lasted out.

There were plenty of other sights to see. A dark man wearing a red turban, like a bandage, round his head, selling bottles of medicine which would cure corns and snakebites. He seemed to be doing a brisk trade, though I never knew anyone in the Borders who had been bitten by a snake. Another man with tattooed pictures on his arms shouted to the crowd to bind him up in clanking chains. He would set himself free no matter how tightly he was tied. And he did, bursting through the chains as if they were silken threads. We applauded him at the end and threw pennies into his hat.

The trouble was how to make the pennies last out, there were so many enticements to lure them from my pocket. Stalls selling coloured sticks of rock, gingerbread men, ice-cream pokey hats, Aunt Sally, the coconut shy. I tried hard to knock down the pile, hoping I might win one to take home to the Dumpling. (What would *he*, a toothless baby, have done with it?) But I always missed. Then Father, an unerring shot, came along, took one swipe and knocked down the lot.

'There, lass,' he said, handing me a hairy coconut. Better still, he fished in his pocket, brought out some coins and replenished my sinking fund.

I sped off, clutching the coconut, towards the shuggy boats. What fun they were! Why did we call them shuggy boats? I have no idea; but there they were, suspended by ropes which we pulled to make them see-saw through the air. Backwards and forwards, higher and higher, till they almost turned tapsulteerie somersaults.

I was not too sorry for the Ewe-Lamb in the boat next to

mine when I heard her wailing, 'I feel sick.' My only fear was that I might lose the coconut.

I saw a group outside Madame Zarah's caravan waiting to have their fortunes told, all looking a little foolish and pretending they were not there. I had not the courage to join them, though I longed to see inside one of the travelling homes. Not to have my fortune told, but to see where they kept their cups and saucers and how they did their cooking. Where was the fire that sent smoke spiralling up the little chimneys?

'Come along, me lucky ladies!'

A dark-eyed gypsy woman with long black hair and dangling earrings stood outside the caravan in her scarlet skirt, calling on the crowd to join the queue. To my astonishment, I saw a familiar figure emerging from the caravan and come stumbling down the steps, her face as scarlet as the gypsy's skirt. The Carthorse!

I remembered it was Liz-Ann's day off, and there she was with a silly-looking expression on her face and her Sunday hat almost falling off her head. I rushed forward to her.

'What was it like, Liz-Ann? What did the gypsy tell you?'

The Carthorse blinked her eyes at me, too flustered to say anything except to gasp, 'Mercy me!' So I could not gather whether her fortune had been good or bad. I caught sight of her lad, George, lurking behind the caravan with a coconut like mine clutched in his hand. So I left them to it and went to look at the menagerie.

The wild beasts were in a big trailer and the man in charge looked the wildest of the lot. A Goliath wearing a leopard skin and cracking a long whip. We cowered past him to peer at the cages. Was that a tiger lying asleep like a big cat? A larger edition of Cinderella. Goliath tried to prod him awake, but the beast only yawned and went back to sleep.

A snake coiled and uncoiled itself in another cage, shooting out its forked tongue. Perhaps the snakebite medicine would come in handy, after all. The monkey was the liveliest of the lot, scratching himself and making funny faces at us. And some coloured birds flew about their cages, battering their wings, poor things, and giving out strange, frenzied calls. I would have set them all free and caged the man with the whip.

I had just enough money left for a final fling on the hobby-horses. As I went whirling round on my painted charger, I could see Jedburgh Abbey nearby whirling with me, and wondered what the monks of old in their quiet cloisters would have made of such a stirring scene.

Suddenly everything had become too noisy, too brash, too highly coloured. I slid off my pony before it slowed down and stood dizzily on the ground, longing to be back in the lonely places far from the throng.

'Sic a dirdum!' I heard an old farmer say as he passed by. 'It wad drive ye oot your wuts.'

So it would. The fair had been fun as a novelty, but it would not do for an everyday ploy. And the travelling folk? How could *they* keep their wuts?

By next day they had vanished off the face of the earth, leaving only the trodden grass behind.

7. Day of Drama

I sensed there was something in the air that morning when Jessie cleared away the breakfast dishes in such a hurry and Liz-Ann started scrubbing the large wooden table with unusual vigour. Jessie was tight-lipped, suffering I thought from the bile, and the Carthorse had a flushed, furtive look on her face.

I was grabbing my satchel ready for my morning dash to catch the school bus when I took a closer look at her. Surely she had never scrubbed the table so thoroughly before. It was not like her to take such pains.

'You've done that *three* times,' I remarked in surprise. 'What's up, Liz-Ann?'

She gave the table a final wipe with the dishcloth before revealing the reason.

'The bairn's gaun to get his throat cut. I mean, his tonsils oot.'

I dropped the satchel and felt my knees giving way. The colour must have drained from my face for the Carthorse looked at me in alarm.

'Jings Geordie!' she cried, clapping the wet dishcloth to her mouth. 'I've went an' let it oot, an' me warned no' to let dab.' But since it *was* out, she told me the rest. 'The doctor's comin' to do the operation on the kitchen table. Puir wee sowl!'

The Dumpling was playing quite happily under the operating table, oblivious of the fate that awaited him. He, too, would have to be rubbed and scrubbed before the dreadful deed was done. I searched in my pocket and found a sweet for him – a jujube – but Jessie came and snatched it out of my hand.

'D'ye want to murder the bairn?' she raged and flung the jujube into the fire. 'He's no' to get a bite afore he's been chloroformed.'

Chloroformed! My knees went even weaker as I pictured the lifeless Dumpling stretched out on the table, the doctor sharpening his knife, the blood gushing. Would the bairn ever come round again? If he died, I would commit murder all right. I would kill the doctor.

'Here, you! get oot ma road.' Jessie was pushing me towards the door. 'Ye'll be late for the bus. Shift yoursel'.'

I took a last look at the Dumpling sucking his thumb for lack of anything better. 'Ch–Cheerio!' I said, and set off reluctantly down the road. There was a lump in my throat big enough for the doctor to cut. I would willingly have sacrificed myself for the bairn.

Mrs Thing was out at the cottage door, not shaking her rug. She was waiting for me with a parcel in her hand. A pair of carpet slippers wrapped in a copy of the *Jethart Squeaker*.

'Ower ticht! Ma bunion's fair stoondin'. Tak' them back, lassie, an' change them for a bigger size.'

I occasionally did messages for the cottage wives. Willingly enough, but today I was not in the mood for Mrs Thing's bunion. I thrust the slippers into my satchel and hurried by, speeding up so that I could catch the bus. But I was not in the mood for that either, or for anything else but thinking about the Dumpling.

I reached the braeface where the hedge of wild apple trees grew. Crab-apples which we called scrogs. From there I could take a short cut, scurry down over the rough grass and make a final sprint to the road-end where Black Sandy would be waiting with the bus. But, instead of sprinting, I slowed down.

'I'm not going,' I told myself and turned back.

I had never plunked the school before, not even the village school where Auld Baldy-Heid was used to pupils failing to turn up, and to their excuses next day. Some legitimate enough, others too lame to pass muster; or, as Liz-Ann would say, to pass mustard. It was easy enough to spot the fibbers.

'Please sir, I had a sair waim.'

'I had to bide at hame to gang to ma Granny's.'

'I had to help wi' the threshin'.'

'Ma breeks needed mendin'.'

'Please sir, I went off the notion.'

Today I had gone off the notion. How could I face Mary-Ann Crichton or concentrate on algebra and Latin while the Dumpling's life was ebbing away? He meant more to me than isosceles triangles. I knew it would not be so easy to hoodwink the teachers at the Grammar School with spurious excuses, but I did not care. I would just tell the truth and they could expel me if they liked.

But I knew it would be no use going straight back home. Jessie would chase me for my life. I contemplated going and hiding in the byre or even the pigsty. Anywhere to be near. Then I looked at the crab-apple trees. I could climb one of the leafiest and sit there undetected. It would not help the Dumpling, I knew, but I could see the doctor coming and going, then I could risk running back home to be on hand if there was an emergency.

Mrs Thing's bunion would just have to stoond. I was

sorry about Black Sandy, though, sitting tooting his horn at Mary-Anne's road-end. He would be worried. I could see him getting out of the bus, looking this way and that, delaying his start till he made sure I was not coming. Would there be time for me to run down and tell him? No; he was climbing back into the bus. A final toot and it moved away. The die was cast.

I settled myself near the top of the tree and hung my satchel on one of the branches. The scrogs were still small and green, but they would do if I was overcome by pangs of hunger, but at the moment they would have stuck in my thrapple. The lump was still there.

I sat so still that a bird – a blackie – came and perched near by me. I watched him waggling his tail and pecking at his feathers. He took a look at my satchel, then at me, but finding neither of us interesting he gave a sad little chirp and flew away. It seemed to me that all the birds were singing sadder songs today. Requiems.

I kept watching for the doctor's car. There was not much traffic on the Jed road, none on our own farmtrack until a shauchling figure turned in. A tramp carrying his bundle on a stick over his shoulder, like Dick Whittington. He stopped to blow his nose without benefit of handkerchief and came shuffling past me, mumbling to himself.

How often they talked to themselves, these homeless wanderers. What about, I wondered. Any time I overheard them it was only a kind of mumbo-jumbo, but it seemed to give them consolation. Dick Whittington was nodding and smiling, as if agreeing with whatever he was saying. At least, he was happy; but then he was not getting his throat cut. I hoped he would not rap at the kitchen door at a vital moment in the operation.

I watched him out of sight, taking his time. Tramps never hurried, conserving their energy for the next step ahead. What was there to hurry for in their leisured lives?

I had taken my eye off the main road and did not notice

the doctor's car till it was almost upon me. Here it came! The doctor sitting in the back, the car rocking as the chauffeur tried to avoid the ruts and loose stones.

A feeling of panic came over me. I had to stop myself from jumping down and holding up the car. 'Stop! Go away! Don't you dare hurt the Dumpling.' But it had swerved past.

And now came the worst part. The long, long wait. I had nothing to do but sit there picturing the scene in the kitchen, exaggerating it in my imagination. The bairn wailing, then silent for ever; Mother wringing her hands; the doctor shaking his head. 'I'm sorry! It's all over. . . .'

I could hear the telephone wires singing over my head. Sending urgent messages for more medicine? A specialist? An ambulance? Suddenly I had such a sinking feeling that I almost fell down from the tree. I ate a green scrog, not noticing how sour it was. There was not even a jujube left in my pocket for consolation.

I had no watch, so it was difficult to judge the passing of time, but presently I heard the purring of an approaching car, a different sound from the clatter of Father's rattletrap. The doctor on his way back. I peered down, half expecting to see him covered in gore, but he was sitting in the back composedly reading the *Scotsman*. Surely he would not have looked so unconcerned if he had killed the Dumpling.

Now I was restless, not knowing what the time was or how soon I dared go back home. Cold, too. There was an icy wind blowing but I had not noticed it before. I started to shiver and could not stop.

Then I heard a familiar whistle. Jock-the-herd was rounding up a stray sheep. When he came near enough I flung a scrog at him. It scored a direct hit.

'Ye wee deevil!' he cried out, picking it up and flinging it back. His shot missed. 'Man-lassie, come doon. It's perishin'. Ye'll catch your daith.'

Never mind that. 'How is the bairn?' I asked anxiously.

'Hoots, he's fine. I ca'd in, an' Jessie tell't me. Come doon, wumman; ye're fair chitterin'.'

The doctor came back next day not so much to see the Dumpling as to examine me. For now, from being too cold I was too hot. I had the high fever and was off school for a fortnight or more.

I have only confused recollections of that strange period when I did see Mother wringing her hands and the doctor shaking his head. But it was Jessie, I am sure, who pulled me through.

Other hands tried to soothe me as I tossed and turned, but it was Jessie's I clung to and her voice I heard through a haze.

'Come on noo, lassie. Pull yoursel' thegither. Lie still an' sleep. Sleep!'

When I had recovered she told me, 'Ye were like a caun'le burnin' oot. An' what were ye ravin' on aboot bunions for? An' carpet slippers?'

They were still in my satchel and I felt I had let Mrs Thing down, but even she had called at the door every day, along with the hinds and the herd, asking anxiously after my welfare. I never knew folk would worry so much about me. I felt I had been silly, lacking in rummlegumption. More so since no one, not even Jessie, gave me a row.

8. The Book of Life

No one in my class at the Grammar School knew what they were going to do when they grew up. Except Lucy, the Ewe-Lamb, who was going to marry a rich man. She would, too.

The word 'career' was never mentioned, and we got no guidance from the teachers. All they said was they were teaching us to face life. What kind of life? I knew what I wanted to do. How to do it was the problem.

Sometimes I wondered what would happen if I went right to the top and sought advice from Mr Archibald, the rector. What an idea! Dafty would never notice me even if I rapped him over the head with a ruler. Nevertheless, I pictured the scene.

'What do you want, idiot?'

'P-Please, sir, I want to be a writer.'

'Stupid ass! Where's your Latin book?'

'Not Latin, sir. I want to write in English.'

'Fool! Get out of my sight.'

It would be hopeless. Teachers, of course, were not really human beings. They were on a higher level. I could not visualize them having any bodily functions, though Dafty did go and shut himself up for long periods in what we called 'the teachers' closet', from which he emerged with a dazed look on his face, smelling strongly of carbolic soap.

As for passing the time of day with me, I would as soon have expected Grumphy the pig to quote Shakespeare.

But one day I had a near miss. It was Saturday. Mother had been baking toddy-scones and her special sponge cake.

'Is somebody coming to tea?' I asked Jessie, who was busy getting out the good cups and giving the teaspoons an extra polish.

'Maister Archie-bald,' she said rubbing away at the sugar-tongs.

She was talking nonsense, of course. Archibald! I stared at her in horror and disbelief. 'You don't mean Dafty from the Grammar School?'

Jessie nodded. 'I tell't ye! Whaur's the tea-cosy cover?'

Never mind the tea cosy. I caught Jessie by the arm. 'Are you sure? Mr Archibald! What's *he* coming for?'

'Hoots! he's comin' for his tea.'

It couldn't be true. But it was. Mother confirmed it. Father had encountered the rector at a meeting of something called the School Board and invited him out to see his sweetpeas. Dafty, it transpired, was a keen gardener.

I was too dumfounded for words. Dafty growing flowers! Dafty coming to see the sweetpeas! Dafty eating Mother's sponge cake!

She had changed into her velvet frock and was giving me a critical glance. 'You'd better go and tidy yourself before he comes. You look a right ticket.'

'No, no!'

Nothing in the world would induce me to take tea with Dafty. Not if I was skinned alive and tortured with red-hot pokers. 'No, no!'

'He'll ask for you,' said Mother, whipping cream for the sponge cake.

'No, he'll not!' Dafty ask for me! 'No, no!'

I would go and hide. Lie low till the danger was past. But before I could dart out of the door, I heard a rumbling sound. A motorcycle and sidecar trundled past the window, scattering cocks and hens out of the way. I took a quick and terrified keek. It was him all right. Dafty wearing a panama hat. I was flabbergasted.

I could not comprehend how he had managed to find his way, turn the right corners and drive up the farm road, instead of going straight on over the Border, never stopping till he reached Land's End. I had never dreamt that he owned a panama hat, far less a motorcycle.

There was a high wall round the rector's house where he lived like a hermit, and a gate through which he disappeared after fumbling with the catch; but it never occurred to me that there might be a garden there or that Dafty could tell the difference between a daisy or a dandelion, even though he might be acquainted with their Latin names.

Father had shaken hands with him and was escorting him to the top garden. Likely, after looking at the sweetpeas, they would have a session in the greenhouse before coming in to tea, but I would be well out of the way by then.

When the coast was clear I scurried outside and ran round to hide in the byre. It was already occupied, though the cows were still out in the fields, by the bantam cock and one of the old crones who visited us regularly. She was sitting on the straw with her few belongings spread out at her side and the remains of a meal she had mooched at the kitchen door. She had taken off her battered hat, jammed the hatpins into it, and was doing up her straggly hair into an untidy knot.

'I've been to the horse trough to wesh masel',' she informed me, taking a clay pipe out of her pooch. She knew, and so did I, that smoking was forbidden in the byre, but I let her puff away. Presently she began muttering to herself, put the pipe out, and lay back on the straw. The banty flew up to the rafters, and I sat picturing the scene in the farmhouse. Dafty taking his tea. Would he drift off into one of his dwams and pour the milk all over the tablecloth?

I was drifting away myself with the old woman snoring beside me when I heard the putter of the motorcycle. A few explosive sounds and it moved off. Dafty was away.

I waited long enough to make certain, then slunk back like a fugitive. Mother was clearing the table and Father, never one to criticize visitors after they had left, was remarking, 'A strange chap, but he fairly knows a lot about sweetpeas.'

'He took a good tea,' said Mother, always pleased when visitors did justice to her baking. Then, as I came in, 'He asked for you.'

'Never!' I could not believe it. She must be making it up.

There was his plate, with a few crumbs from the sponge cake left on it. Fancy Dafty taking a good tea like an ordinary human being. I could not get over it, and took a slightly different view of him from then on.

But a few days later when I met him face to face in the school corridor with no hope of retreat, he brushed past me without noticing my existence. So things just went on as usual.

Who, then, could help me to become a writer?

I asked the Dumpling for want of anyone better, but he only gurgled and gave me a toothless smile. All he wanted was to play clap handies.

'You wait,' I told him. 'I'll write stories for you.'

I had already scribbled some down in an old jotter. A copybook with wise axioms in perfect calligraphy on the top line. 'He who hesitates is lost', contradicted on the next page by 'Look before you leap'. *I* hesitated long enough to find a pencil with an unbroken point and then leapt.

My handwriting and spelling did not match that of the top line, but I strove to capture the style of the tales Jessie told in the byre, and to recapture the ones I had made up out of my own head. Stories I had told to keep Elsie, the grieve's wee girl at Swinside, quiet when she lisped, 'Elthie wantth a thtory.'

But these were just homely tales of the farmyard, about Grumphy the pig, about tattie-bogles and bubblyjocks. Who in the outside world would want to read them? I must puzzle my brains to create characters like Mr Micawber or Long John Silver, but I knew nothing of the kind of life *they* led. There were no Mr Micawbers in the Borders.

Strangely enough, it was the moudie man who set me on the right road.

The moudie man had been hired to rid the farm of moles. Moudies, they were called in our part of the world. He hung their pathetic little carcases in rows on the fence once he had caught and killed them, and I scowled at him every time our paths crossed. 'Cruel thing!' I hissed under my breath.

The moudie man lived in the bothy, Jock-the-herd's headquarters, occupied on occasions by such itinerant workers as the lambing man or the drainer. He cooked for himself after getting supplies from the vanman. Succulent meals of sausages, ham, and herring fried in oatmeal, and strong tea brewed in a tin teapot which he boiled on the fire. I sometimes sniffed an appetizing aroma as I passed the bothy on my way to or from my castle on the hill.

One day I found him sitting outside, leaning against the lintel, finishing off an alfresco meal of bread and cheese. I averted my gaze from the row of dead moles hanging from the fence, and was about to pass by when he called out in a friendly voice, 'Hullo! What's that ye've got under your airm?'

That was my copybook. I was on the way to my fortress to get some peace from Jessie, who kept raging at me for sitting scribbling at the kitchen table when she wanted to scrub it.

'Can ye no' stop scartin' wi' your pencil an' do something usefu'?' she scolded, brandishing the scrubbing brush as if about to hit me with it.

What was useful?

I had mastered the skills of milking a cow, turning a heel, baking a scone, looking after the Dumpling, washing the dishes, kirning the butter. Writing and reading were not useful. They had no end product. As yet! Wait, Jessie, wait! Give me time and peace to fill my copybook.

'It's just a book,' I said to the moudie man, trying to hide it from him.

'What kind o' a book?'

'It's a storybook.' I wanted to pass on, but he was in a conversational mood. He took out his pipe and began cutting up some thick, black tobacco.

'A storybook, eh? I'm a great reader masel'.'

'Oh!'

I looked at the moudie man with a little more interest, trying not to think of his murderous mission. He was ordinary enough, like Tam or Wull, dressed in old corduroys and a torn jacket. But, right enough, there was a different look in his eyes, as if his head might be full of visions.

'What kind of books do you read?' I wanted to know.

'Och! it's no' *books*,' said the moudie man, cramming the tobacco into his pipe. 'Just the book o' life.'

'What's that?' I asked in surprise.

He looked around him, giving a wide sweep with his arm to indicate what he meant. 'It's a' aroond ye, lassie. I read it every day an' never get sta'd.' (Sta'd meant sated. Fed up.) 'There's aye a new chapter. Scenery,' he went on. 'Ay, an' folk. A'body I meet. They're a' in the book o' life. Ye're in't yoursel', lassie. Read it an' ye'll never get sta'd.'

As I walked away up to the castle I felt like one of

Blackie's kittens whose eyes were beginning to open. I would take a closer look at the scenery on my doorstep, at the real-life characters I met every day and write about them. No need to invent Jessie. She was better than Mr Micawber. And what about the moudie man himself?

But when I put pencil to paper, underneath 'The early bird catches the worm', the inevitable thing happened, as it did with all my stories. He turned into an animal. It was a mole I was writing about, not the moudie man.

'Once upon a time there was a little wee moudiwart who lived with his Uncle Geordie underneath the ground. . . .'

Still, he smoked a pipe and wore baggy corduroys, like the moudie man's. And later on he became part of a collection of children's bedtime stories published in a book. So maybe the moudie man did me a good turn.

At least, I continued to turn the pages of the book of life every day, even when helter-skeltering down the farm road to catch the school bus. Sometimes I read the sky. There was a lot to see up there, though it was risky to run and gaze heavenwards at the same time. Often I fell over my feet and landed flat on my face.

It was the clouds that fascinated me. Some days they looked dark and dangerous, scudding across the sky as if chasing angrily after each other. On sunny days they were as fluffy as cottonwool tinged with pink, billowing out like clean washing.

Down below there was always plenty to read. The cottage wives with stringent comments to make as I scurried by their doors. 'Losh! she's like a steam engine!' A weasel running across my path. A hedgehog sitting by the roadside, poking out his soft snout. He, too, would appear in the bedtime book later on. The trees, with a different aspect about them every day, particularly when their leaves were turning russet red. And always the hills, far off or near, depending on the changing weather.

Oh! there was a lot of reading in the book of life.

I wished I could write about Father without turning him into a seahorse or a centipede. Better still, that he would write his own tales instead of just telling them; though how could they be improved by putting them on paper? It would be difficult to put a funnybone in print.

He was a great one, Father, for being the first in everything. Today he would have booked a trip to the moon; and what a tale he would have to tell when he came back. He had the first motorcar in the district, the first wireless set, the first electric light, though the generator broke down so often we always kept the old paraffin lamps ready in the background, the first golf course, rough and rabbit-holey though it was. Soon he would have the first tennis court.

And now it was the first tractor. The hinds would have nothing to do with it at first, so it was left to the Boss and *he* was not sure how to make the best use of his new toy. The carthorses shied at the sight of it, and the men called it a muckle noisy beast, though not the kind of beast they could control. Father did his best to teach them the rudiments of starting, stopping and steering; but no amount of 'whoaing' and 'gee-upping' would make the muckle noisy beast go straight.

Through a gate, for example. I had always suspected both Tam and Wull were short-sighted. Or long-sighted, maybe. Even when they borrowed the herd's specs they could never manoeuvre the new-fangled monster through a narrow opening without coming to grief. So it was left to the Boss to do his best, or his worst. At least, his exploits with the tractor added to his fund of funny stories.

'You should have seen Jock-the-herd louping over the dyke like a collie. He was sure I was trying to run him down.' Father chuckled at the memory of Jock taking to his heels and scampering out of the tractor's path, yelling, 'Man-Maister! gie me time to say ma prayers!'

Jock never did take to the tractor. It was the one thing he refused to mend when it broke down, except to give it a vicious kick as he passed by. Sometimes that did the trick!

It was a new ploy for Father. He extolled the tractor's virtues to his farming cronies, though what the virtues were, I was not sure. Certainly, when the tractor went, it went faster than the carthorses. 'Haud on, maister!' The men would run breathlessly after it when Father set off at such a lick they could not catch up on him. Its greatest virtue in their sight was its frequent breakdowns, leaving them to return peacefully to their reliable Clydesdales.

The tennis court was the idea of my elder brother and sister to enliven the long holidays from their colleges in Edinburgh. They were accustomed to team games, not the solitary pastimes I pursued with a burst ball, the pig's bladder, or an old iron gird. Swinging on a gate, jumping over the corn stooks, skipping with a frayed clothes rope, were pursuits beneath their dignity. My brother sometimes tried to organize games of cricket. I was always a fielder.

'Run and fetch that ball,' he ordered in a lordly manner.

I spent ages on all-fours retrieving it from under the reaper in the cart shed, or extracting it from the water barrel. Until the worm turned and I shouted defiantly, 'Run and fetch it yourself!'

Stunned silence. Then, 'Who do you think *you* are?'

Somebody, I said to myself. So there!

Laying out the tennis court involved heated arguments, since no one was sure of the right size or where to find a flat enough location for it. But at length it was decided to use a stretch of ground in the upper meadow; and after scything the long grass and levelling it, more or less, with the heavy garden roller, it was ready for marking out with white-wash, a job that had to be done each time we decided to play. A frayed net was erected in the middle, and Jock-the-herd, grumbling about 'A waste o' guid grund', set to with hammer and nails to put up some wire-netting round the court to keep out the cows.

I picked up the rudiments of the game from my elders and betters. More difficult to pick up a racquet. Only the gentry from Edinburgh had the right equipment. The rest of us played as we could with warped ping-pong bats or old badminton racquets found in the garret. But gradually we amassed enough second-hand gear to invite friends to come and sample the delights of a home-made tennis court. I was lucky to get a game at all, and was always left out if company came; but in the end I could play as well as the rest, often barefoot or in my stocking soles.

Mother always played with her hat on and did not run about the court. She just stood still and hit the ball if it happened to come in her direction. Father could be classed as a spirited player, hitting unorthodox shots which often foxed his opponents into protesting, 'That's not fair!'

I was surprised at the lack of sportsmanship amongst the grown-ups, how they hated to lose, and at their violent disputes about the score.

'Out!'

'No! In! It hit the line.'

'Did not!'

'Did sot!'

They would argy-bargy for ages.

I lacked the competitive spirit and did not much care whether I won or lost. I liked the running about, the jumping over the net to change sides, and the occasional direct hit I managed to score on a sulky opponent; but I could not stand the petty squabbling which constantly held up the game.

One day I surprised myself and everyone else by throwing down my racquet, stamping my bare feet and shouting, 'Shut up and get on with it!'

They were so astonished that they did.

It was another chapter, I suppose, in the book of life.

9. Forget-me-not

Postie! Postie!
Bring me a boon.
A letter, a postcard,
A line frae ma loon.
Postie! Postie!
Hasten your feet.
If ye pass by ma windy,
I'll sit doon an' greet.

Our postie had flat feet, but there was no need for us to sit doon and greet, for he never passed by our window. Where else could be go? There was nothing but hills beyond the farmhouse.

When Jessie heard him coming she swung the black kettle on the swey over the fire so that she could make a pot of tea to refresh him after his long walk. He left his bicycle at the herd's hoose and took a short cut across the fields, climbing over fences and dykes with his heavy bag thumping against his back.

It was not the mail that made it heavy. More often it was filled with 'messages'. Obligements which the postie had done for isolated country wives, who relied on him as their only link with the outside world. Bring me a boon meant fetching boots from the cobbler, medicine from the chemist, matching wool, taking a broken clock to be mended, buying a new scrubbing brush. A dozen odd errands which the postie uncomplainingly undertook after cycling back to town when he had completed his country round. Little wonder his feet were flat; but we never once heard him grumble.

Of course, it was give and take. The grateful wives saw that he was well supplied with eggs and butter; and when they were making jam they put a pot aside for the postie. Fadges, spare-ribs and pigs' puddings all found their way into his mailbag, so that it was never empty, either coming or going.

When he came into our kitchen he was thankful to heave it off his back and deposit it on the table before sinking with a sigh into his favourite chair. Then he stooped down to loosen his bootlaces while Jessie poured out his tea. In between sips he unfastened the straps of his bag and rummaged inside to find any mail addressed to Overton Bush. Bills and circulars for Father, a copy of the *Scotsman*, perhaps a picture postcard for Mother. Seldom anything for me.

Except on one red-letter day, though it was not a letter he brought out, but a small intriguing parcel with my name on it. Postmarked Hawick. So it must be from Auntie Bessie and Uncle Tom.

'Open it oot, wumman,' said the postie, who was in on all our secrets; and not only ours, for he made a point of reading every card, examining each postmark, and assessing the contents of any parcels. But we never considered him nosey; he just liked to know! And the information he gathered was often useful to pass on to some of his cut-off customers, eager to hear any scrap of news. That the minister's cousin was coming to visit him, that the Scotts had received a parcel from Dundee, (a soft parcel which felt like a jumper), that Mary-Anne had been sent an official document, something to do with her pension, that a card addressed to Camptown had gone all the way to Cape Town by mistake. Fancy that! And come home to roost by a roundabout route, with goodness knew how many post-marks on it. Such items of news were meat and drink to country folk starved of social contact.

It was such a rare event for me to get a parcel of my own that I could not wait to undo the knots, but seized the scissors to cut the string.

Jessie slapped me down. 'Na, na, lassie! Ye'll end up in the puirhoose.'

It was a waste of time unravelling the knots but the postie helped me and at last I unearthed the contents. A neat little box with a jeweller's name on it from the High Street, Hawick, and a note written partly in Auntie Bessie's round hand and partly in Uncle Tom's scratchy script.

I laid the letter aside and opened the box. Nestling in cottonwool lay a little blue brooch made of enamel and mother-of-pearl, shaped like a forget-me-not. Specially for me.

'We thought it would match your eyes,' wrote Auntie Bessie. Mercy! Never mind eyes; I liked the brooch. It was nice; the nicest thing I had ever possessed. I pinned it on there and then and the postie said, 'Ay, it sets ye,' meaning it suited me. He gave the Dumpling a ride-a-cock-horse on his leg before lacing up his boots and hoisting his mailbag over his back.

"A'weel, that's me awa'. Mind an' write to the folk in Hawick to thank them.'

I did. I wrote a long letter. Two pages, oozing gratitude for the unexpected gift, telling them how I would treasure it and that it would always remind me of Hawick. Forget-me-not. I even treasured the wee box after rescuing it from the Dumpling who was trying to stuff it in his mouth. And I had a keek at my eyes in the looking-glass to see if they were the right colour, and so they were. I had never noticed them before.

As for the brooch itself, I wore it every single day to school pinned on my jersey under the neckline of my gymslip so that the teachers would not notice it. I fingered it lovingly now and again, feeling a warm glow, knowing it was there. Something private of my own to cherish.

But one day the Ewe-Lamb noticed it and eyed it with envy. Lucy, who had everything she desired, except the forget-me-not brooch.

'Oh! that's nice! I'd like to have one like that. Where did you get it? Will you let me try it on?'

'No, I'll not!'

I felt fiercely possessive about the brooch. It was *mine*.

Day in day out, the Ewe-Lamb pestered me. 'It would go with my new tussore-silk frock. Will you not lend it to me?'

'No, I'll not!'

She did everything but snatch it from me. Even bargained. 'Look! how would you like a new pencil case? I've got two. You can have the red one if you let me have the brooch. It's as good as new.'

'No!'

I was adamant. She tried me with pearl beads, a bracelet shaped like a serpent, a ring with a stone missing, tortoiseshell clasps for my hair, a plush velvet purse; but I would not budge. For once I was one up on the Ewe-Lamb.

Not for long.

We were to have a new classmate. The boy from London. Miss Crichton and the other teachers stressed that we must be kind to him for he had lost his parents. They were not dead, I was relieved to hear, only gone to India, which seemed as remote as heaven. In their absence, Norman was coming to stay in Jedburgh with his Aunt Janet, a maiden lady who lived in one of the large houses on the outskirts with a turreted roof and a garden hedged with boxwood on which sat neat rows of clipped cockerels. Miss Janet and her gardener were for ever clipping at them. Topiary, I found out it was called.

For a maiden lady, Miss Janet looked very gentlemanly. She wore gaiters and spats, and strode around in a shapeless tweed costume sagging at the hem. Or drove about in a dog-cart with a long whip in her hand. I never saw her whipping the pony, but I always kept well into the roadside in case she might whip me. She had that look about her; but maybe it was just a look and she was quite nice inside. Like a hard caramel with a soft centre.

'Peety she couldna be flyped,' as Jessie would say. Flyped meant turned inside out.

We all pitied the laddie from London coming to live in such a forbidding household, but as it turned out we need not have worried, for it soon became evident that Norman had the knack of finding his own feet. In no time he had his Aunt Janet eating out of his hand.

Soon it was he who was driving the dog-cart at a spanking pace, he who was clipping the box-hedges into more imaginative shapes, he who let a breath of fresh air into the turreted house and lit up his aunt's life till she grew less manly, even to the extent of discarding her spats and gaiters.

What was it about Norman that attracted people to him and made Miss Janet his slave? There was nothing special about his appearance. He was small and wiry, with lively brown eyes and a turned-up nose. Ordinary enough, but with more personality, more verve and dash than the other raw boys I had hitherto met. Whatever it was, there was something about Norman that left its mark on us all.

Even on that first day at school when we were all feeling a trifle uneasy, ready to make allowances for the new boy and go out of our ways to make him feel welcome, it was Norman who took hold of the reins, as he had done with his aunt's dog-cart. He assessed the lot of us, it seemed, with one glance from his quick brown eyes. You, you and you! Yes! I can see what *you*'re like. I'll get on all right with you all.

He did.

It took longer for me to assess him. At first I thought he was too self-assured, almost cocky; but it was just that he was aware of his own abilities. They were there for all to see. He could speak better French than Miss Crichton, he was quick at solving mathematical problems, his essays were streets ahead of mine, and when he spoke I liked the way he put words together into rounded sentences, like someone in a book talking.

Of course, the other boys mocked his English tongue, but instead of taking offence he mocked them back in a put-on Border accent. 'Hoots-toots! dinna be daft.' So they got on all right.

The one thing Norman did not shine at was games. He sat on the playground wall instead, reading a book. That intrigued me. And he sometimes wrote in a little notebook, which intrigued me more. I longed to know if it was a story, like the ones I was trying to write. But when Norman spoke to me it was not about stories.

It was about the Ewe-Lamb.

The boy from London had fallen under Lucy's spell, and made no bones about showing his feelings for her. Just as he never hid his light under a bushel, he was open in his admiration for Lucy, who was as pleased as punch to have captured his attention and blossomed under his compliments.

The other boys never looked at any of us twice, not even once, preferring to kick footballs around the playground. But here was a devoted swain following Lucy around like a puppy, bringing her little presents of fruit and flowers from his Aunt Janet's garden, and telling her he thought she looked beautiful.

Fancy! It was enough to turn any girl's head. No wonder Lucy went about with such a self-satisfied smirk on her face. She had won first prize. And done it deliberately, too. I had watched her at the beginning making a dead set at Norman. She flattered him, fluttered her eyelashes at him, hung on his every word, invited him home to tea and told him she thought *he* was wonderful.

So that was how it was done! I might have learnt a lesson from her, but I didn't. Her tricks worked, but the more I saw of them the less I liked them. So I took avoiding action to keep out of Norman's way, but the boy from London was so besotted he felt he must talk to someone about the Ewe-Lamb's virtues. For some reason he chose me.

'Isn't she a picture?'

'Uh-huh!'

'She's so kind and good.'

'Uh-huh!'

'Don't you think her curls are lovely?'

'Uh-huh!'

One day while Norman was extolling the Ewe-Lamb's virtues he noticed the forget-me-not brooch I was wearing.

'Oh! that's nice,' he said admiringly. 'It reminds me of the colour of Lucy's eyes.'

True enough, they were bluer than mine; but I never liked the forget-me-not brooch after that. And the next time Lucy asked for it I handed it to her there and then.

'What?' said she, surprised and delighted. 'Can I really have it? What do you want for it?'

'Nothing. You can keep it.'

So she did, but *I* kept the wee box.

It was soon after this that Norman changed his tune and transferred his affections to me. Too late. I would have none of him.

Just as I had watched the Ewe-Lamb's attempts to

ensnare him, I now saw the disillusionment setting in. She was too sure of her conquest. She expected him to be at her beck and call, to trot after her, to fetch and carry, and never to take his thoughts off her for a moment. Most of all she resented the times he sat on the playground wall with his nose in a book, neglecting her.

'Come on, Norman,' she would say, tapping her foot imperiously. 'I'm waiting. I want you to carry my satchel.'

For a time he went meekly enough, but there were too many 'I wants', and as the weeks went by he followed her more reluctantly.

Then one day he sought me out and, instead of singing Lucy's praises, started to criticize her.

'Don't you think she's a bit selfish?'

'M-m!'

'Nothing much in her head, has she?'

'M-m!'

'Always wants her own way. I'm getting fed up with her.'

'M-m!'

I would not commit myself, but when he started to pay *me* compliments, I sidestepped.

'I think you're the most intelligent girl in the class.'

'Me!'

'You're not selfish. You've got such a kind heart.'

'Away!'

'I like your red hair, even when it's untidy.'

'Jings!'

After that I took even less trouble with my tousled locks and would not prink or preen to attract his attention. Besides, my affections were still firmly fixed on Fatty, Mr Smith, the science master.

Fatty was growing plumper by the minute, expanding in all directions till his waistcoat would scarcely meet, let alone fasten; but still I had a fond motherly feeling for him, almost the same as I felt for the Dumpling. And, when the boys tried to get a rise out of him, he looked so bewildered and vulnerable that I longed to protect him from their thoughtless pranks. He took no notice of me, of course, except to tell me how hopeless I was at science. The most intelligent girl in the class, indeed!

I would sooner have had a compliment from Fatty than from the boy from London. Still, it was difficult to ignore someone with such a strong personality, especially when he talked to me about books. That caught me. It was the first time I had been able to converse with anyone on the subject. Norman had read so much – far more than I had – but occasionally we could meet on common ground and I could forget my inhibitions and became animated as we discussed our favourite characters. Then I would hastily withdraw as he tried to slip me a compliment, or when I saw the Ewe-Lamb pass by, tossing her curls in high dudgeon, furious with me for taking up Norman's attention.

I never confessed to him that I hoped to become a writer myself, though I was tempted when he showed me what he was writing in his notebook. Poetry. He read some of it to me. As good as the Ettrick Shepherd's, I thought, though Norman's was less about birds of the wilderness, more about thoughts, moods, feelings. One I noticed was entitled 'Lucy', but he had drawn a line through it and never read *it* out. I blushed scarlet when he said he had written one about me, and ran out of earshot rather than listen to it.

So we had an uneasy relationship. Unlike the Ewe-Lamb, I never sought Norman out or laid any claims on him, but for the rest of his stay in Jedburgh he remained constant to me. I knew at the back of my mind there was some sort of spark between us, but I was afraid to fan it into flames.

It never rains but it pours! I was not exactly besieged by suitors, but about this time I discovered I had another 'follower', though I did not recognize him as one at first.

What on earth was the matter with Big Bob? He had taken to hanging about at Mary-Anne's, lurking behind the dyke till the school bus came and deposited me at the road-end.

The big laddie was at an in-between stage, having left the village school where he had made little progress and taken a job as an orraman on a farm (an odd-job man) prior to becoming a fully-fledged hind. He was broadening out, his voice had deepened, and there was the hint of a moustache on his upper lip. His breeks were too short and his arms protruded from his jacket sleeves. He wore clumping boots and his hair was more unruly than mine. Altogether not a prepossessing sight to greet me as I stepped off the bus.

'What are you doing here?' I asked crossly, prepared to dodge out of his way in case he got up to his usual bullying tricks. Pulling my pigtails, tripping me up, or pushing me into the ditch.

'Nothing,' said Big Bob, sheepishly.

'Well, away you go!' I said, and away I went.

But he was there again the next night, with his face washed and his hair combed. I stared at him in amazement.

'What's up? What do you want?' I asked suspiciously.

Big Bob gulped and held out his hand for my satchel. 'I'll . . .I'll carry it for ye.'

'You'll do nothing of the sort,' I said, snatching it back. Likely he would swing it round and hit me on the head with it. 'Away you go!'

I marched down the road, quickening my pace when I heard his boots clumping behind me. What the dickens was he up to now? I went faster and faster, hoping to shake him off, but Big Bob kept stolidly on. It was not till I reached our farm road-end that he gave up.

'Ch-Cheerio!' he called in his cracked voice; but I did not respond, and went hurrying home, wondering what to make of it.

Throughout the day I forgot all about Big Bob, but every night there he was, kicking his heels, waiting to follow me down the road like a shaggy sheepdog. It was disconcerting, and one night I turned on him in a temper and shouted 'Shoo!' as I sometimes did to the bubblyjock.

It had no effect. Big Bob had a thicker skin than the bubblyjock and no amount of rejection would put him off. Gradually he sneaked up on me and we marched side by side, not speaking. What was there to speak about? We had nothing in common. I was a superior person with a knowledge – a smattering, anyway – of Latin, French, maths, Shakespeare. No use talking to Big Bob about books. He had flung his away the moment he left school, and it was doubtful if he would ever open one again. Catch him writing poetry!

If anyone hove in sight he nipped over the dyke or through the hedge and emerged when the coast was clear to take up his position by my side. Even so, his antics were noticed. I was highly incensed one night when Mary-Anne said to me, with a twinkle in her old eyes, 'I see your lad's waitin' for ye doon the road.'

'He's not my lad!' I said indignantly, and was even crosser than usual to my escort.

It was a strange courtship, if that is what it was. In the end, I hardly noticed him; and what did *he* get out of it, apart from giving me a playful dunt now and again? Occasionally he brought me an offering. An apple, a pandrop that had lain about in his pocket for long enough, a ribbon which he must have bought from a tinker, or more likely filched from Cathie, his younger sister.

Sometimes we got back on our old terms, quarrelling as we used to do at the school behind Auld Baldy-Heid's back, and I would hit out at him as we argued back and forth.

'I did not!'

'Ye did sot!'

If it was a courtship, it was hardly up to the standard of Liz-Ann's novelettes.

But all this was as nothing compared with the great event

that put everything else in the shade. For now my first story was printed and I had become a real author. Upsides with Charles Dickens and Sir Walter Scott. Or more likely Anon, for the story was unsigned; not even my initials at the end. But it was *my* story, word for word, printed in a magazine for all to see. I was a writer.

It was an unpretentious little religious magazine called *Morning Rays,* badly printed and with the pages so loosely stapled that they often fell apart. It came out monthly and was handed free to all the children in the Sunday School, which I still attended at Edgerston kirk before the big service began, helping the smaller fry to find their places in their hymnbooks, wiping their noses, and picking up the collection pennies they dropped in the pews.

Apart from its Bible lore, *Morning Rays* always carried a story, a sickly tale with a moral standing out a mile. Rubbish! I thought when I scanned it every month. I could do better myself. So I sent one in.

I copied it out carefully in my best handwriting on clean pages torn from my school jotter and looked up doubtful words in the dictionary, like receive – the 'e' before the 'i'. The story, naturally, was about an animal, and it, too, had a moral, but not such a pointed one as the others. It was called 'The Selfish Squirrel', but by the end of the story Sandy (the squirrel) had seen the error of his ways and become *un*selfish. There was a drawing of a squirrel as a heading, so I was illustrated as well as printed.

I could not believe my eyes when I saw it. It had been such a long time since I sent it in, to an address I discovered on the back page of *Morning Rays*. I was so overcome that I almost stopped breathing and could not sing 'Day by day the little daisy' when the minister gave it out.

I was in two minds whether to shout to the whole world, 'Look! that's my story,' or to keep the secret to myself. When I took the magazine home I opened it at my page and left it lying about, but nobody noticed it. I toyed with the idea of taking it to the Grammar School and showing it to Norman, but it would be small cheese to someone who wrote poetry. So, though I would have liked a pat on the back, I kept quiet about it. But *I* knew.

Nothing could stop me now.

10. The Tishy-paper Dress

'What deevilment have ye been up to noo?' Jock-the-herd shouted to me as I perched perilously on a rickety washstand in the garret and stuck my head out of the skylight window. 'Man-lassie! are ye no' ower auld to be shut in the gaol?'

No!

Advanced though I was in the ways of the world – a scholar, a literary light, a *femme fatale* with swains at her feet – I was still only a wee lassie at heart, lacking in rummlegumption and subject to grown-up control. Though I now 'spoke back' and resisted authority, there were times when my elders got the better of me.

This was one of them.

'Man-lassie! what did ye do?' the herd wanted to know.

'Nothing!'

That was it. A sin of omission, and for once I could see the justice of my sentence. It was like Alfred and the cakes. I had completely forgotten to watch the potatoes bubbling in a big pan on the fire while Jessie was out feeding the hens and gathering the eggs.

The pan was no longer bubbling by the time she came back, and I was sitting at the kitchen table with my head in a book. *Jane Eyre*. Not only were the potatoes burnt to cinders but the pan was ruined.

'Ye're a useless hussy!' raged Jessie, giving me a cuff on the ears. 'Up to the garret wi' ye!'

I could have defied her, I suppose, but old habits die hard, so I meekly allowed myself to be marched upstairs. Jessie almost flung me into the garret and before turning the key, shouted, 'Ye can redd up the place for your sins. It's in a terrible slaister. An' ye'll get nae tatties for your denner the day.'

And no dinner either, if she forgot to let me out.

True enough, the place *was* in a slaister (a mess) as I saw when I climbed down from the washstand after exchanging greetings with the herd, but who wanted a tidy gaol? I liked the familiar clutter. Cobwebs hanging from the ceiling, a pile of musty books spilling over each other in a corner, a rocking-horse that would no longer rock, the banjo without a twang left in it, the dressmaker's body leaning drunkenly against the wall. Best of all, the wooden kist full of cast-off clothing.

I had rummaged in the old chest often enough when looking for garments to clothe the tattie-bogles. It was like Pandora's box, there was no knowing what would come to light. Feather boas, a moth-eaten fur coat, a shoulder cape covered with black beads, a straw basher, long lace gloves, satin shoes with pointed toes.

Sometimes I dressed myself up, sometimes I dressed the body. She looked quite human in a tattered skirt and blouse with a straw hat perched on her head.

There were men's clothes, too, in the kist. Old blazers, plus-fours, frock coats and bashed bowler hats. I remember – how could I forget? – the day I dressed myself up in what must have been somebody's Sunday best in bygone times.

The trousers, of course, were far too big for me, but I found a pair of galluses (braces) and anchored myself in with the aid of a few safety pins. Then I put on a dickey (a starched shirt-front) and a cutaway coat and shoved a lum hat on my head. I must have looked a real ticket. The body gave me a blank look and seemed to slump sideways.

To add the finishing touches, I found a false moustache, a pair of elastic-sided boots and a cane; and was swaggering about like Beau Brummel when there was a rattle at the garret door.

My gaoler come to release me.

'Come doon! There's a veesitor wants to see ye.'

'Oh no! I can't come just now.' I called back. 'I'm not dressed. I mean, I'm too dressed! Wait, Jessie, wait!'

I tried to struggle out of my galluses but it was hopeless. Meantime Jessie was shouting, 'She canna wait. Come doon! It's the laird's leddy.'

'Oh jings!'

If it had been Queen Victoria it could not have been worse.

The laird's lady was an ageless, exquisite, doll-like creature made of porcelain, not flesh and blood, seldom seen out in the wide world and never without being dressed to perfection in pastel shades of mauve and pink, with gold glittering at her throat and perfume on her dainty handkerchief. She was like some princess in a fairytale – the princess and the pea, perhaps – who lived on a higher plane than the rest of us and had never experienced anything common in her life.

I had often looked at her admiringly, like a cat looking at a queen, never spoken to her. She was miles above me in every way; and now she was waiting at the door in her carriage, with the coachman on the box and Mother standing by looking respectful. What on earth would she make of me, dressed like a dafty?

There was no escape. 'Come on, wumman! Stir your stumps!' Jessie was shouting to me.

She went downstairs in front of me and did not notice what I was like till I emerged through the front door and tripped over my trousers as I made my way to the carriage.

Mother gave me a horrified glance, and the laird's lady raised her lorgnette to take a closer look. The best I could do was brazen it out and tip my top hat to her.

'How quaint!' she said to Mother in an amused voice. 'Isn't she quaint?'

So that was what I was! Quaint! The laird's lady gave me one of her sweet smiles, shook out her frilly parasol and drove away, waving a little gloved hand.

'I'll quaint ye!' stormed Jessie, grabbing me by my coat-tails. 'Ye've disgraced yoursel' an' the hale faimly. Awa' back to the gaol an' think black burnin' shame o' yoursel'.'

Poking about in Pandora's box was like turning the pages of an old diary, bringing faded memories back into focus. When I came across a wooden sword I burst out laughing, recalling the time when the hinds made their unwilling debuts on the stage as extras in one of Father's amateur productions.

The play had something to do with Robert the Bruce and the men were needed as warriors. All they had to do was stand like stookies on the stage and shout.

'What'll we shout?' the hinds wanted to know.

'Just shout *HO!*' said Father.

Tam and Wull cleared their thrapples. '*H-HO!*' they shouted more or less in unison. It sounded terrible. Petrified with stage fright, their knees as well as their voices were shaking.

'I wish I was oot spreadin' muck,' groaned Tam when

they were dressing up for the performance in ragged kilts, with their long drawers rolled up above their knees.

'Me, tae!' said Wull, peering out from under his helmet. 'What is't we're to say again, Tam?'

'*H-HO!*' said Tam, word perfect, though paralysed with fear.

I was behind the scenes as a kind of wardrobe mistress, and had a great struggle buckling on their armour, and a greater struggle pushing the men on to the stage when the crucial moment came for them to make their entrance.

Wull promptly dropped his sword, so I had to poke my hand through the curtains (Mary-Anne's bedroom ones lent for the occasion) and pick it up for him, earning a round of applause for my pains. Which was nothing to the cheers the hinds received when the audience recognized them.

'Mexty! that's Tam! An' that's Wull! Gie them a clap.'

The men were so taken aback they could only whisper their shouts. 'H-ho!' as if they were mice rather than warriors, but Robert the Bruce (who else but Father?) stepped into the breach and 'Ho-*HO'd!*' for them.

I tried to tug at their kilts to remind them to exit when the time came. They gulped out an extra '*HO!*' and got a great clapping of hands before clattering backwards down the wee steps that led off-stage.

The sweat was pouring off their faces after their ordeal, and as they discarded their helmets and rolled down the legs of their drawers, 'That's me feenished wi' the stage,' announced Wull.

'Never again!' agreed Tam. 'Thon's purgatory.'

But they spoke about it in the work stable for long enough afterwards.

'D'ye mind the time we said *HO*?'

'Wull I ever forget? *HO!*'

It was a kind of password between them for ages.

As I put the warped wooden sword back into Pandora's box, I pushed old memories aside and came back to present-day problems. The invitation I had received that morning from the Ewe-Lamb, a formal printed invitation the postie had brought.

It was a fancy card in a fancy envelope. Indeed, everything about it was fancy, even the occasion. A fancy-dress party. That is what I was being invited to attend at Lucy's house. Carriages at 11.00 p.m.

Fancy!

I knew fine the Ewe-Lamb did not really want me at her fancy party. She wanted Norman, along with other favoured schoolfriends, but she must have suspected it would be easier to get him if she invited me as well. It was not difficult to see through her.

'I'm not coming,' I told the fancy invitation and gave it to the Dumpling to play with.

But, just for the fun of it and to while away my term of imprisonment, I began to dress myself, mentally, from the contents of the old chest. How would Lucy like it if I stuck on the false moustache or blackened my face and appeared as a minstrel with the banjo under my arm? I could easily enough dress as a tattie-bogle, or I could wear a wig and a false nose so that no one would recognize me. Nothing pretty-pretty. Leave that to Lucy. Not that it would matter, since I wouldn't be there.

Of course, there was the tishy-paper dress. It lay at the bottom of the kist amongst the mothballs, carefully wrapped in tissue paper, which Jessie called 'tishy'. It was the one thing I was forbidden to touch; it was so delicate it would fall apart, but of course I had taken a keek at it in the past, but never ventured to open it out of its wrappings. All I could see were flounces of lace and ivory silk. Someone's discarded ballgown, perhaps. More suitable for the laird's lady than for a gawky schoolgirl.

Nevertheless, I did more than keek at it today. Greatly

daring, I lifted out the tishy-paper and revealed the contents. After how many years?

As I shook out the dress it billowed around me like hawthorn blossom. I could smell the faintest hint of perfume mingling with the stronger aroma of mothballs. The dress was frayed in places, discoloured in others, and creased where it had lain folded for so many years. But it was still beautiful, the most exquisite gown I had ever seen. There was a lovely little wreath of silver leaves to go with it.

I longed to see someone wearing it, so I carried it carefully to the dummy and dressed her up in it. She looked a treat with the silver leaves round her head. I could imagine the Ewe-Lamb eyeing it with envy. It was a shame to hide it away in tishy-paper.

'You look like what's-her-name in the fairytale,' I told the body. 'The Snow Queen.'

I was aware of the telephone ringing downstairs. Presently there came a thump on the garret door.

'Come doon!' shouted Jessie. 'Ye're wanted on the tellyphone.'

'Me?'

Who on earth could want to speak to *me* on the telephone?

It was Norman. He did not beat about the bush.

'I say, have you got an invitation from Lucy to a fancy-dress party?'

His voice sounded more English on the telephone, almost like the laird's. I could scarcely understand him.

'Y-Yes,' I replied.

'Oh, good! Then I can accept it. I wasn't going to go, unless you were coming, too.'

'I'm not keen,' I told him.

'What? I beg your pardon.'

It was Norman's turn not to understand me. He did not know what not being keen meant.

'I'm not coming,' I said, putting it more plainly.

'Oh, but you must,' insisted Norman. 'I tell you what, I was thinking of dressing up as Robin Hood. Why not come as Maid Marian?'

'I'm not keen,' I repeated. Certainly not keen to dress up as Maid Marian. That would make us a pair.

'Come on!' coaxed Norman, putting on his most persuasive voice. 'It could be great fun. But not without you. That would spoil the whole thing. You will come, won't you?'

'I . . . I'll see. But I'm not keen. . . .'

Father drove me to the party. I felt foolish sitting beside him in the motor, toshed up in the tishy-paper dress with the wreath of silver leaves round my head, long lace gloves on my hands, and satin slippers on my feet. For once not a hair out of place. Jessie and Mother had brushed and braided it till all the highlights were shining.

'She looks no' bad,' Jessie said, giving me the accolade. Equivalent to winning first prize at a cattle show. 'I've seen worse.' But if I had been flyped – turned inside out – she would have seen a different picture. For two pins, and there were plenty holding the tishy-paper dress together, I would have got out of the motor if it had stuck and run back home, satin slippers and all. But for once Tin Lizzie purred her way down the road without a hiccup, and far too soon for me we reached the town.

'Right, lass,' said Father, depositing me at the Ewe-Lamb's door. 'I'll pick you up at eleven. Enjoy yourself.'

In the interval he would go to a place called the club to play billiards with his cronies. I think he was glad of a night out on his own. I wished I could go with him, but the club was only for men.

The door was opened by a maid in a lace cap and apron, the very opposite of the Carthorse. A confusion of chatter and laughter met me as I was ushered into a bedroom where the bed was heaped with wraps, and some of the girls in my class were titivating in front of the mirror. They were dressed up as witches, fairies, Little Miss Muffets and Red

Riding Hoods, and all had brought parcels with them, presents for their hostess. Oh dear! I had not thought of bringing anything for Lucy.

'Who are you supposed to be?' whispered Jeannie, one of my classmates, dressed as Little Bo-Peep and obviously, like myself, in a state of jitters.

'I'm not sure who I am,' I said, taking off Mother's cloak which she had lent me for the occasion. 'It's just an old frock.'

Robin Hood was hovering about in the passage outside, neat in his green tunic, with a bow and arrow in his hand.

'I *say*!' he gasped when I emerged. 'That's beautiful!' It was the tishy-paper dress he was talking about, not me. I hoped it would not fall to pieces before the evening was out.

The Ewe-Lamb's mother gave me an appraising glance and said, 'Come along, dear. Here's Lucy. Isn't she looking lovely?'

Yes, she was. Lucy had pulled out all the stops and was dressed as an angel in a flowing robe, with gauzy wings, and a glittering halo round her head. A sight to behold. All golden curls, flushed cheeks and angelic looks. Till she saw me.

'Where did you get *that*?' she said sourly, eyeing the tishy-paper dress with displeasure.

'Oh! it's just an old thing I found in the garret.'

'Isn't it beautiful?' said Robin Hood unwisely.

'Huh!' said Lucy, tossing her curls. 'What do you think of mine?'

'Lovely!' I said hastily. 'You look like a – an angel.' I noticed she was wearing my forget-me-not brooch.

The Ewe-Lamb preened and fluttered her eyelashes at Norman, while I looked around, trying to recognize the rest of the guests under their disguises. The boys stood around uneasily with their false beards askew, dressed as pirates, cowboys and highwaymen. Robin Hood, I had to admit, was the most swashbuckling of the lot.

Lucy's father, got up in a mask and a cloak, called us into the big sitting room where the furniture had been cleared to make room for games and dancing. We were served with fruit cup with which we had to toast the Ewe-Lamb who stood in the centre, looking a perfect picture. One flap of her wings and she would fly off to paradise. But she stayed with us.

I would have been content to sit in a corner and watch, alongside Little Bo-Peep who clung to me for comfort, but we were all forced to participate in the games that followed.

We were in-betweens, a little too old for Hide the Thimble or Drop the Hankie, not sophisticated enough for grown-up games, whatever they were. So, while Lucy's mother played the piano, we bumped around at Musical Chairs and the Grand Old Duke. I kept tripping over the tishy-paper dress, aware of pins dropping from their moorings, my hair growing dishevelled and the silver leaves skew-whiff on my brow. But the Ewe-Lamb remained perfect throughout.

Her father did some magic tricks, making pennies disappear up his sleeves and bringing a real rabbit out from under his cloak. Then her mother cried, 'Take your partners!' and struck up 'The Rosebud Waltz' on the piano. The girls sat still, trying not to look hopefully across at the boys who had segregated themselves at the other side of the room.

When I saw Robin Hood coming in my direction I gave him a don't-you-dare look and hissed 'Lucy!' at him. She was looking at him expectantly. He must dance with his hostess first. Whoever was to be a wallflower, it must not be the Ewe-Lamb.

I waltzed with a ghost who kept muttering desperately, 'One-two-three-*turn*! One-two-three-*turn*!' Thank goodness he did not attempt to reverse. Then I did a polka with a pirate whose sword came between us. By the time Robin Hood claimed me it was a Highland Scottische, which he had never heard of before, far less danced.

I did my best to steer him in the way he should go and to stem his breathless attempts to pay me compliments.

'I say! I think you're looking absolutely. . . .'

'No, no! That's the wrong foot! *Hop*! Now twirl!'

All the hopping and twirling had made us hungry. But soon we were invited into the dining room where the table was spread with so many good things to eat it was difficult to know where to start. We had to line up, take a plate, and help ourselves.

'It's a boo-fay,' the Ewe-Lamb informed us proudly.

Jeannie was lingering shyly at the end of the queue. I went back to lend her support and was standing outside the door when I heard a scuffling sound. Thinking it was the kitten I had given Lucy, I set off along the passage to have a look at her. But it was no kitten I came face-to-face with; it was an old man, 'cruppen doon' as Jessie would say, almost bent double with his humpy back, shuffling out of the kitchen in his carpet slippers, peering about him to see what he could see.

'Hullo, lassie,' he said in a furtive whisper. 'What's gaun on?'

'It's a party,' I told him.

'A pairty!' He gave a wheezy cough. 'Och weel! I'd better keep oot the road. They'll no' want me to disgrace them. Them an' their pairties!'

Just then an angry angel came fluttering along, almost spitting with rage.

'Grandpa!' she hissed, grabbing him by the arm and turning him about. 'Away back to the kitchen at once! Go on! Keep out of the way!'

She pushed him towards the kitchen door, and as he shuffled meekly away, she turned to me. 'What are *you* doing here?'

'I'm just waiting in the queue,' I said lamely.

By now Jeannie was coming along the passage to look for me. The Ewe-Lamb fixed her halo more firmly on her head and gave her a sugary smile. 'Come along, both of you, and have something to eat. It's a boo-fay.'

As I nibbled a small sausage roll I reflected that even angels keep skeletons in their cupboard. We ended with pink ice-cream, some of which dropped on to my tishy-paper dress and did it no good; but by now it did not matter, for everyone was looking more relaxed, less starched. False noses had fallen off, seams had split, stockings were wrink-led, and I was not the only one to resort to safety pins. The boys were in a more bouncy mood when we went back into the other room to continue the festivities.

Little Bo-Peep shrank closer to me when they started a fiendish game called Forfeits, in the course of which we were all called upon to 'do' something, if only to bow to the wittiest, kneel to the prettiest, and kiss the flowers on the carpet. The Ewe-Lamb was in her element when she re-ceived more than her fair share of attention and when her turn came to do something, stood on a little footstool holding out a bunch of artificial violets, and sang 'Won't You Buy my Pretty Flowers?' in such a beseeching voice it brought tears to her parents' eyes.

It was a good enough game if one could have just sat and watched the others making fools of themselves, but I longed to escape to the kitchen and keep the wee old man company when the dreaded moment came for me to be pushed into the centre and told to 'perform'.

'Come along, dear,' said Lucy's mother in an encourag-ing voice, tinged with impatience. 'Do something.'

All I could do was stare at the pictures on the wall. Dozens of them, all of the Ewe-Lamb at different stages from her christening onwards. Then I caught a distorted reflexion of myself in a little round mirror. Was I as dim a vision as *that*?

'Come on, lassie, pull yoursel' thegither,' I seemed to hear Jessie's voice admonishing me. 'The back's aye made for the burden.'

I straightened mine. 'I'm going to recite,' I announced in a shaky voice.

There was a Border ballad in my mind, about Bonnie George Campbell. It ended sadly as all such dirges did.

> Saddled and bridled and booted rode he,
> A plume in his helmet, a sword at his knee.
> But toom cam' his saddle all bloody to see;
> Oh! hame cam' his guid horse, but never cam' he.

No! I'll not do it, I said to myself! Never mind the old Border ballads. I'll recite a new one. Norman was not the only person who could make up poetry. Mine was in broad Scots, so he would not understand it, but never mind; I would do it.

'Go on, lassie,' Jessie was urging me. 'Do your best.'

Yes, Jessie, I will!

The poem, naturally, was about an animal. A wee kirk moose – a church mouse who had difficulty finding anything to eat in church, except an odd peppermint someone had dropped in a pew.

> 'There's naethin' much to eat
> Except the paraphrases
> Or a hymn book for a treat.
> I've eaten the Auld Hunner,
> I've chowed Beatitudes,
> But I canna say I've found them
> Just the tastiest o' foods. . . .'

The poem ended with a plea.

> 'So, I'm hopin' that some Sunday
> Wad ye mind aboot me, please,
> An' bring me in your Bibles,
> Just a wee bit taste o' cheese?'

As I finished I looked at the mirror. The reflexion was not so dim now, but it seemed to be Jessie there, not me, nodding approval.

I got a polite handclap from the company. Robin Hood did not applaud at all, but he came to my side.

'Who wrote that?' he asked.

'Anon,' I lied.

But I could tell from the look in his eyes that he knew.

Father was in a mellow mood on the way home, singing songs at the pitch of his voice.

'Many brave souls are asleep in the deep. . . .'

But I was wide awake after all the excitement.

The tishy-paper dress was never the same again, neither was I. Not only had I made my debut in society, I had overcome another hurdle. Fancy standing up and spouting my own poetry in public!

11. Facts of Life

'What's up with Liz-Ann?' I asked Jessie one day, and got a typical Jessie answer.

'Up? Huh! Mair likely doon!'

I was so taken on with myself and my own affairs, particularly with a magic letter I had received from the BBC ('We like your story and hope to broadcast it soon in *Children's Hour*') that I had not noticed something was happening to the Carthorse. But gradually I became aware that there *was* something.

I tried to fit the jigsaw together to solve the puzzle. It was something not immediately discernible; just that her spirits seemed to be veering from hysterically high to lamentably low. Usually the Carthorse was on a more or less even keel. Low – Jessie was right – rather than high. But now she was as changeable as a weather vane. One moment I would hear her singing cheerfully at the kitchen sink, usually a good-going hymn. 'Shall we gather at the river?'

'Yes!' sang Liz-Ann lustily, as she wrung out the dishcloth, 'we'll gather at the river. The beautiful, the beautiful, ri-i-ver. Gather like the saints at the river. . . .'

She could raise the roof when she was in full voice.

Half an hour later I would notice – when I noticed her at all – that the singing had stopped, that Liz-Ann's nose was red and her eyes swollen with weeping. No use asking her what was the matter, she just lifted up her apron and hid her face in it.

Of course, I had seen the Carthorse weeping and wailing many a time before. She had a ready supply of tears and could turn on the waterworks at the drop of a hat, or more likely a scolding word from Jessie.

The Ewe-Lamb had the same facility but, whereas Liz-Ann looked a blotchy mess when she was crying, Lucy seemed touchingly pathetic. She used her tears as a trump-card, letting the dewdrops trickle one by one down her cheeks, leaving her blue eyes awash and her long lashes dripping, at the same time giving out sad little sighs calculated to melt the hardest of hearts. Except mine. Even the stern Miss Crichton caved in and let Lucy off tricky French verbs if they proved too much for her sensitive pupil.

'There, there! Don't worry, dear. Dry your eyes.'

There was no one to say 'There, there!' to the Carthorse, but I did try to act as a buffer between her and Jessie. And, after observing her varying moods for a week or two, I could bear it no longer. I must find out.

That day I had heard her singing loudly, if not tunefully, as she peeled the potatoes. Another of her favourite hymns.

> 'Jesus bids us shine
> With a pure, clear light,
> Like a little candle
> Burning in the night.'

Good! I thought. She's in one of her skyhigh moods. But, wait! will it last?

No!

The hymn came to an abrupt end. I heard the potato peeler being flung down and Liz-Ann bursting into a loud fit of sobbing, the worst ever. This was it! I ran into the back kitchen and caught hold of her as she crouched over the sink sobbing as if her heart would break.

'What is't, Liz-Ann?' I shook her as if trying to shake the answer out. 'Come on, tell me. Has Jessie been rotten to you?'

The Carthorse shook her head. There would be nothing new in that. Jessie was always rotten to her.

'Well then, what's wrong?' I had to know. It was time to put an end to this nonsense. If it wasn't Jessie, it must be George. Had he let her down? Jilted her? I hardly dared ask. The Carthorse would not understand the word jilted, so I put it into plainer terms.

'Is't George? Have you cast out?'

Another shake of the head, more violent this time. So that was all right. But it made the problem more puzzling. What else could it be?

Suddenly Liz-Ann wiped away her tears with the back of her hand and blurted out her bombshell. The exact opposite of being jilted.

'Me an' George, we're gettin' spliced.'

The bomb hit me in the midriff and knocked the wind out of me.

'Spliced!' I gasped when I got my breath back. 'You mean you're getting married?'

'Yes!' cried the Carthorse, as if she and George were about to gather at the river. Her tears had vanished and there was a blissful look on her face. On mine, too, as the news sank in. I gave a great whoop of joy and danced her round the back kitchen.

'Hooray!' I cried, whirling her past the pigs' pail. 'That's great news, Liz-Ann. Great!'

At last the Carthorse's dreams would come true and the

contents of her bottom drawer see the light of day. The long cotton goonie with coarse lace at the edges, the tray-cloth embroidered with clumsy lazy-daisy stitches, the knitted teacosy cover, and all the odds and ends she had collected during the time she had been going steady with George. Wooden spoons, a ladle, a tin teapot, sundry jugs, vases and egg-cups.

I continued to dance her around until we both grew dizzy. And then I was aware that the strange thing had happened again. The wind had changed and Liz-Ann's laughter had given way to sobs. I wondered if she was going off her head and if we should send for the doctor.

I held her tightly. 'There's nothing to greet about, Liz-Ann. You and George are getting married. What more do you want?'

The Carthorse shook me off and burst into another fit of boo-hooing. Then she dashed past me and went clattering out of the kitchen door, leaving the potatoes unpeeled and me more puzzled than ever. But determined to get to the bottom of it.

When Jessie appeared from the parlour with the dustpan in her hand I tackled her straight out.

'What's wrong with Liz-Ann?'

'That article!' she said contemptuously. 'Her!'

'Yes, her! She's getting married, isn't she? So what's she bubbling about?'

Jessie brushed the dust – the oose, she called it – from the dustpan into the fire, and as the flames shot up, she turned and gave me a look.

'She's got plenty to bubble aboot. She *has* to get married.'

'Has to?'

'For the sake o' the bairn.. Silly eediot!' Jessie pursed her lips in disgust.

The bairn! I was so dumfounded I had to sit down on a kitchen chair before my legs gave way.

'D'you mean Liz-Ann's . . . expecting?'

Jessie nodded grimly. 'Glaiket gomeril!', which was even worse than silly eediot. '*I* wad hae sorted her, but the mistress is that soft she's lettin' her bide on for a bit till she an' that silly sumph get settled. A fine pair they'll mak'.'

They would be more than a pair. There would soon be three of them. My mind was running round like a hobbyhorse. Fancy the Carthorse, glaiket gomeril though she was, having such a secret life! Knowing all about *that*! I knew little about that myself except from whispered conversations mingled with giggles from some of the girls at the Grammar School. And I had seen things, of course, on the farm; but that was animals, not human beings. It was a strange carry-on whichever way one looked at it.

How had Liz-Ann learnt about it, and how had she and George ever got close enough to do it? They were more often apart than together, she walking behind while he wheeled his bicycle in front.

It was the strangest thing; I could not get over it. When the Carthorse came back into the kitchen I looked at her with new respect. She knew!

I jumped up and seized her by her rough red hands. 'Congratulations, Liz-Ann,' I cried, 'I've heard about the baby.'

She was in an in-between stage, half tearful, half smiling. She blushed scarlet when I spoke to her and did not know whether to give way to tears or laughter. But, when she saw I was pleased with her news, she was pleased, too. And suddenly her plain face took on such a blissful look, she seemed almost beautiful.

I had a thousand questions to ask her. I wanted mainly to know about *that*, but she wouldn't tell, apart from saying, 'I just fell,' whatever that meant. So I asked her about the baby instead. Did she want a boy or a girl?

'A wee lassie,' she said with a broad smile. 'But I'll tak' what I get.' Indeed, she would have to.

Her face clouded from time to time and the waterfall of

tears flooded her eyes as she recalled some of the stormy scenes she had suffered. The poor thing must have gone through many trials and tribulations since her sinful secret had been discovered.

Yet it was, after all, no great disgrace. Liz-Ann's would not be the only love-child to be born in the district, and at least *she* was getting married. There were several women living in the neighbourhood with no wedding rings on their fingers, bringing up bairns without the aid of a father. I had been to school with some of them and none of us thought they were different. We were all made of the same mould.

I was curious to know how George had popped the question. 'Did he go down on his knees?' I asked Liz-Ann.

'Oh no! naethin' like that. The idea! He just said he wad stand by me.'

Well, good for George!

The upshot was they were to live with her parents in the roadman's cottage till they found a place of their own. If ever.

'We're to get the back bedroom,' said the Carthorse, her face aglow at the prospect. I could see she was already furbishing it in her mind's eye with the contents of her bottom drawer. 'The mistress says she'll lend us the creddle. The Dumplin's oot o't.'

I had forgotten about the baby. As yet there were no bulging signs to be seen, but the Carthorse was so lumpy already, it would be difficult to tell the difference.

'What about a honeymoon?' I asked, not sure of the ethics of such a ploy in the circumstances.

Yes, she and George were going on a honeymoon.

'M'Auntie Bell's invited us to Galashiels for the weekend.' Her face was aglow again. I hoped with all my heart that M'Auntie Bell would do everything she could to make it a memorable weekend for the newly-weds.

In the days that followed there was more singing than

sobbing to be heard. The disgrace was fading into the background, and we were deafened with 'Rescue the Perishing' and 'By cool Siloam's shady rills'. George was even allowed to call at the kitchen door, though Jessie would never let him over the doorstep.

'I'm havin' nae cairry-ons in ma kitchen.' As if he might murder us with the bread knife.

Yet, though she still rounded on the Carthorse and called her a glaiket gomeril, there were times when Jessie showed the softer side of her nature. For example, when Liz-Ann was about to pick up a heavy pail of coals.

'Pit that doon, ye silly eediot! Ye'll do yoursel' a mischief. I'll cairry it.'

In due course the Carthorse acquired her greatest treasure, an engagement ring. It had once belonged to George's granny, whose knuckles must have been less swollen than Liz-Ann's. It was a nice wee ring with a ruby-coloured stone in the centre, but no amount of manoeuvering could force it on to Liz-Ann's engagement finger; but, not to be beaten, she wore it proudly on her pinky and kept polishing the stone with her apron till it shone like a real ruby, as perhaps it was.

There was the tricky problem of what the bride was to wear at the wedding, which was to be held at home in the roadman's cottage, and to which we were all invited.

'Couldny get spliced withoot the hale jing-bang,' she told us affectionately. She would have included the Dumpling and Blackie the cat, if she could. 'But what'll I pit on?' she puzzled. 'I'll need to wear *something*.' Too true.

I wished I could lend her the tishy-paper dress, but she would have burst its seams just by looking at it.

'Were you thinking about white?' I asked, trying to picture the Carthorse in a madonna-like gown with a sheaf of lilies in her arms.

'Mexty no!' she cried, giving the ruby ring on her pinky a vigorous rub on her pinny. 'I daurna!' She flushed. 'No' in *ma* state. It'll need to be a costume, I can gang awa' to Gala in't.'

So a costume it was, shapeless like Liz-Ann herself, and puce-coloured. Mother gave her a frilly blouse to go with it, and I saved up to buy her a cheerful string of pink pearls. 'You'll look a treat,' I told her, though I had my doubts.

'D'ye think I should pit on a veil or a hat?' she pondered.

'Why not both?' I said lavishly.

So she wore a straw hat, pink like the pearls, and a floating veil with which she wiped her eyes now and again during the ceremony when emotion got the better of her. She looked not bad.

Father gave her some folded banknotes as a nest-egg and dressed himself up like a gentleman going to a society wedding. Lum hat, flower in his buttonhole, cutaway coat, gloves and all. I would have married *him* like a shot.

The real bridegroom looked as if he was about to go to his execution, tightly buttoned into a navy-blue suit, with a collar almost choking him and a face that grew redder as the ceremony proceeded.

Jessie was there, with a jet brooch in her blouse, after protesting, 'It's no' worth dressin' up for sic a pair o' useless gowks.' Not all that useless. At least they knew how to make a baby.

The only other wedding I had attended had also been in a cottage, in one of the hinds' houses at home, but I had been too young to enjoy it and missed all the fun by falling asleep before the merriment began. Not this time. I missed nothing.

We were all squashed like kippers into the room – the ben-end of the house – and sat or stood where we could. The ceremony itself was mercifully brief. The bride and groom just stood up before the minister, who opened his Bible and said his piece. It was the only time I had seen Liz-Ann and George so close together. George forced the wedding ring on to her finger and the deed was done.

We all sang 'The Lord bless thee and keep thee,' though I think the Carthorse would have preferred 'Shall we gather at the river', and George, by the look of him, would sooner have been shot. But after the final blessing everyone relaxed and congratulated the happy couple by pumping their hands up and down. Father went further and kissed the bride soundly on her veil. Then the bridegroom loosened his collar and everyone made for the door to witness the ceremony of 'running the braes'.

This was an old Border custom held after every cottage wedding, when the young males of the company set off at a gallop to run a measured distance, the winner receiving a large silk handkerchief and a kiss from the bride. As well as the prospect of being the next in line to be spliced.

We all gathered at the door to watch them set off. There was only a handful of them, so few that Jock-the-herd, being a bachelor, was pressed to join the fray. 'Ready! Steady! *Go!*' shouted Father, and they were off. I cheered my favourite, Jock-the-herd, but it was Big Bob who came lumbering home first. The bride flourished the silk handkerchief at him and tried to kiss him on the nose. He, in turn, tried to present me with the handkerchief, but I would have none of it. Then we all crowded back into the cottage for the wedding feast. Steak pie followed by wedding cake and shortbread.

Tongues as well as waistcoats were loosened. Father toasted the newly-weds in a comical speech. It was too much to expect George to reply, but as least he gave a gulp, like a fish out of water, and we all clapped, his bride louder than any.

It was nice seeing the Carthorse so happy. 'You look lovely,' I told her, and she blushed and bloomed. Even George's tongue, under the influence of his mother-in-law's home-made wine, was loosened to the extent of him remarking, 'It's a great do, is't no'?' I think he would have enjoyed himself thoroughly but for the thought of going off to M'Auntie Bell's at Gala.

I admired Father. He was in fine form, and kept the party rolling with his quips and songs. Even Jessie held her fire and forbore to reprimand the bride when she skited her cup off the table. 'Tuts!' cried Jessie, and left the rest unsaid, graciously accepting a second glass of wine.

I had a sip or two of the potent brew myself. It was nicer than lemonade and had no effect on me. So I thought until we went to wave the happy couple off – Father was driving them to the train in Jedburgh – and found my legs wobbly.

'Man–lassie! ye're tiddly,' said Jock-the-herd as I lurched into him.

'Am I?' I said woozily. 'It's nice.'

Someone had tied a pair of old boots to the back of the motor. We all threw rice and confetti at the couple. The Carthorse was so overcome by it all that she was laughing and crying hysterically at the same time. Her hat was skew-whiff and she had to support her bridegroom who was leaning at an angle like the tower of Pisa. But as the car set off, with the boots dangling and us cheering like mad, she leant out and shouted happily, 'Ta-ta! I'm fair whummled!'

Which said it all. George had been right. It was a great do.

The farmhouse kitchen was quiet without the Carthorse. Too quiet. Certainly there were fewer breakages, but I missed her clumsy clatterings, and I think Jessie missed someone to rage at, so I received more of the rough edge of her tongue.

'You're a terrible tyrant,' I told her one day when I was in a defiant mood.

'Me?' said Jessie, as if the idea had never entered her head. 'Ye're haverin', wumman. Wring oot that dishcloot.'

'No, I'll not! And you are so a tyrant. Have *you* ever had a telling-off?'

'Mony's the time.' She squeezed out the dishcloth herself as if she was wringing my neck. 'I used to get ma character every day frae the mistress. No' your mother. She's ower saft. In ma first place.'

'Did it do you any good?'

'Did me nae hairm.'

'But d'you not think it's sometimes better to be soft, Jessie?'

'No!'

She was an immovable object, Jessie. Hard as nails. But the soft centre was there all the same.

In due course another raw lassie took the Carthorse's place. The exact opposite of Liz-Ann. Pale and colourless, afraid to say boo to a bubblyjock, easier for Jessie to knock into shape. A mousey type. In fact, she eventually earned the nickname of 'the Moose'.

I did not take to her, maybe out of mistaken loyalty to Liz-Ann, maybe because there was something about her I could not fathom. Something *sleekit*. She was not straight-forward like the Carthorse, but had a sly underhand way of putting the blame on someone else.

'*She* done it,' she would whisper to Jessie behind my back.

It was not long before Jessie discovered that the Moose, like all mice, had sharp claws which she unsheathed when she was in a tight corner.

'But she'll no' get the better o' me,' declared Jessie, an expert at setting mouse traps. So the pair of them had many a scratching match, and I kept out of the contest as much as possible.

But I did miss the Carthorse.

I knitted a pair of little socks for the baby who arrived safely, not all that long after the honeymoon. A wee lassie. So Liz-Ann's wish came true. I had high hopes she might name the baby after me. But she called it Jessie. Wee Jess.

Fancy that!

12. Secrets

We all had our secrets. How to hide them was the problem.

Father in the greenhouse absorbed in his own ploys amongst the seedboxes, Mother who retreated now and again to the spare room, ostensibly to tidy the wardrobe. One of the drawers was locked. I wondered if she kept *her* secrets there. Even the Dumpling had private chuckles to himself, and the new servant lassie was full of sly mysteries. Liz-Ann had tried to conceal hers till nature gave the show away.

Mine was that letter from the BBC hidden in my school-bag from prying eyes.

And what about Jessie's?

One day she startled us by announcing out of the blue, 'I'll no' be comin' in the morn.'

Mother was ironing her best blouse, goffering the frills at the neck, and I was sitting at the kitchen table pretending to do my homework, but the hated Latin grammar was hiding one of the Carthorse's discarded novelettes.

I had been reading a particularly purple passage. ' "My darling!" he breathed, taking her in his strong arms and raining hot kisses on her ruby lips.' Jings! was this how George and the Carthorse carried on?

When Jessie spoke Mother looked up in alarm.

'Are you feeling ill?' she asked anxiously.

Unlikely. Jessie did not believe in illness. 'I'm fine,' she said sharply. 'Joo-anne'll be in.'

Her sister Joo-anne only came in when there was an emergency. Sometimes she worked out in the fields as a bondager, but mainly she stayed at home in the herd's hoose, cooking their plain meals, washing, mending, knitting Jock's socks and long black stockings for herself and Jessie.

She was nice, Joo-anne, but so withdrawn it was difficult to get through to her. Partly because of her deafness, partly on account of her stammer. I was never sure how deaf Joo-anne was. At times she could pick up a whisper or hear a far-off whistle, yet it was almost impossible to converse with her at close quarters. So she was just left to get on with her work in her own silent world.

I knew she had something Jessie did not possess, and that was a funnybone, for sometimes I saw her shaking with laughter. Perhaps at some comical idea that had come into her head. I felt sure she and Father would have got on a treat if only they could have communicated.

Though Joo-anne looked elderly to me, she was treated as the shy younger sister in the herd's family, the one who had to be shielded. Yet, when she was forced out of her shell, she could don her bondager's bonnet and take her place in the harvest field, keeping pace with the men; or put on a clean pinny and cope with the farmhouse kitchen when a crisis arose. She was plumper than Jessie, a little softer, with white hair that looked as if it wanted to curl.

She came in promptly that morning, silent as ever. The porridge was ready and the kettle boiling when I came down to eat a hasty breakfast before setting off to catch the school bus at the road-end.

'How's Jessie?' I asked in a loud voice.

'She's f-f-fine!'

I went off to school with the mystery unsolved, but the puzzle buzzed about in my head all day, and I tried to unravel it instead of concentrating on my lessons. If Jessie was not ill, why had she not come in as usual?

It was one of Mary-Ann Crichton's conversational days. During the lesson we were supposed to talk to each other in French, so we did not talk much, just a few stilted sentences.

'*Comment allez-vous?*'

'*Je suis* fed up. *Comment allez*-vous?'

Miss Crichton's catarrh was at its worst and so was she.

'*Elle est dans un* rotten temper, *n'est-ce pas?*'

She kept blowing her nose and drying her hankies on the radiator, one of her less endearing habits. Then she would snort, and shout to us when our conversation dried up.

'*Parlez! Parlez!*'

So we parled as best we could to our neighbours sitting at nearby desks. '*Je pense que . . . que je suis* scunnered.'

'*Moi aussi.*'

Norman leant across and parled a lot of nonsense at me. I pretended not to understand it. Nearing the end of the lesson, and after another blast of nose-blowing, Mary-Ann's watery eyes lit on me.

'*Vous! Venez ici!* Come on! *Vite!*'

What now? Please let her not make me address the class in French, or repeat that awful piece of poetry about Monsieur Corbeau and the Fox. Anything but that. I wished I knew how to burst into tears, like the Ewe-Lamb.

Miss Crichton fumbled in her pocket and brought out some money which she thrust at me.

'*Mouchoirs! Papiers.* Buy me some at lunchtime. I can't get out to the shops. *N'oubliez pas. Des mouchoirs papiers.*'

I had never bought paper hankies before, but jaloused the

newsagent in the High Street might stock them, along with the *People's Friend,* the *Squeaker,* the *Scotsman* and sundry pens and bottles of ink.

'*Avez-vous des mouchoirs papiers?* I mean, paper hankies!' I asked him when I rushed in, intent on fulfilling my mission.

Luckily he did not hear the beginning of the sentence, his attention being focused on a more important customer. The Ewe-Lamb purchasing some coloured transfers. Lucy had so much pocket money she was always buying this and that. Her parents were good customers and the newsagent was giving her full attention.

'There you are! I've put them in a nice bag for you. My regards to your father and mother.'

As she brushed past me on her way out, he turned his attention to me. 'Paper handkerchiefs, did you say? I think I have a packet somewhere.' He did not trouble to put them in a bag, just for me, but anyway I got them. That was the main thing.

The Ewe-Lamb was lingering at the door, sniggering to herself as she stared at someone across the street.

'Look at her! You can tell she comes from the wilds.'

I came from the wilds myself and was in no mood to join in Lucy's sarcastic merriment. Besides, the upright figure across the way looked all right to me, though her costume was of an old-fashioned cut, her velour hat of no particular shape or style, her black boots stout and clumsy. She carried a reticule over her arm, and doubtless looked different from the smarter shoppers in the High Street. But at the sight of her my heart gave a happy thump.

'It's Jessie!'

The Ewe-Lamb turned her supercilious gaze on me.

'Good gracious! do you know *her?*'

I was about to say she was our servant when I changed my mind.

'She's my best friend,' I cried, and skedaddled across the road to clutch Jessie by the arm.

She turned and gave me one of her straight looks. 'What's up?' she asked in an expressionless tone.

That was the question I wanted to ask *her*. What was Jessie doing here in the middle of the big town in her good costume and her Sunday stays? I could hear them creaking as she moved; and what was she carrying in her shabby reticule?

At a quick glance I could see only a bunch of flowers, hardy yellow and purple irises that grew in the garden behind the herd's house. Anything that grew in that exposed patch had to be hardy; but why had Jessie picked them and where was she taking them?

'What are you doing here, Jessie?' I ventured to ask.

'Mindin' ma ain business.'

I tried again, puzzled as to how she had transported herself from the wilds to the High Street.

'How did you get here, Jessie?' Surely she could not have walked all the way. Or borrowed Jock-the-herd's bicycle.

'By the brake,' she said briefly.

No elaboration. But, of course, I knew what the brake was. A ramshackle conveyance which picked up passengers from the country and took them on a long slow journey to town. Formerly it was horse-drawn. Now it was a bus; an old rattletrap which Jessie still called the brake.

It came out as far as Camptown on certain days – though nothing was very certain about it – stopping at various road-ends on the way and finally dropping passengers at the marketplace in Jedburgh. There were no recognized stopping places. Folk just stood out in the road when they heard the rattletrap coming and waved Andy to a standstill.

He was an easy-osy character, Andy, blissfully unaware of the passage of time, willing to loiter for a crack with the postie or any of his cronies he encountered on the way. Ready, too, to do obligements. So there was no knowing who or what might be inside the brake.

A chiming clock on its way to be repaired, a child to be

delivered to her granny, a sack inside which something moved and squealed. A piglet, maybe. Andy would go out of his way up side roads to oblige a farmer who wanted a piece of broken machinery collected. And he might return to the main road by a roundabout route, leaving would-be passengers stranded along the way.

It was a hitty-missy way of getting about, but for want of anything better it served its purpose. There was no certainty when Andy would start back on his outward journey. When the spirit moved him and when all his errands had been accomplished. Andy made his own timetable.

But at least he had brought Jessie to Jedburgh, though for what purpose I could not find out. She did not seem anxious to prolong our meeting.

'Ye'd better get on, lassie, or ye'll be late back,' she said, dismissing me.

So away I went with Miss Crichton's *mouchoirs* clutched in my hand, but I took a backward glance, not for the purpose of spying on Jessie but just to make sure she really was there.

She looked such a lonely figure I almost ran back to join her, but I knew that was not what she wanted. As I watched, I saw she was making her way to the old abbey kirk. And it suddenly came into my mind that maybe she was going into the churchyard to place her flowers on one of the neglected graves, but that was only a guess.

Somehow I did not feel in tune with the singing lesson that afternoon. 'Little brown jug' and 'A-hunting we will go' sounded too jolly for my mood. I mouthed the words, but my voice, far less my heart, was not in them. My feelings were more attuned to the sad sagas Miss Paleface made us learn in her poetry lessons.

> She turned her back unto the room,
> Her face unto the wa'
> And with a deep and heavy sigh,
> Her heart it brak' in twa.

The Latin lesson taken by the rector at the end of the afternoon did little to lift my spirits. Except that he was not there; at least, not in essence. Dafty's body was seated behind his desk like a waxwork figure, but he might have been a million miles away for all the notice he took of us. We had to keep a wary eye on him, though, for who knew when the statue might stir to life and start bellowing at us?

The half-dozen boys with whom I shared the privilege of the irascible rector's tuition all treated me like dirt. (Except Norman who had joined the class when he came from London, and who passed me little notes which I never read.) The others involved me in their kicking matches under the desks and made me the target of their catapults. Sometimes we played cheating games of noughts-and-crosses, often ending in violent whispered arguments. And sometimes the boys tiptoed out of the room, one by one, leaving me alone to face the rector's wrath.

Today I ignored the boys and joined Dafty in a dwam. About Jessie. What had she been doing all afternoon? Was she still wandering round the abbey churchyard or had she gone away home in the brake?

Neither Dafty nor I stirred till the closing bell jangled. None of us had done a stroke of work.

'Idiots!' he shouted, startled out of his reverie. 'Do you not hear the bell?' He glared ferociously at us. 'Off you go, you donkeys, and be sure to do your homework.'

'Yessir!'

We were up on our feet and off like whippets, fighting to get first through the door. I ran helter-skelter to the school gate, hoping to get the seat next to Black Sandy in the bus. I was too late; someone was already sitting in it. An angular figure, her back as straight as a ramrod.

'Jessie!'

She looked down at me from her great height in the bus. I could tell she was thinking what a sight I was, with my tousled hair and wrinkled stockings, but she made no comment, apart from: 'Sandy's givin' me a lift oot. I missed the brake.'

I went and sat in the back with the rest. We usually squabbled all the way home, but with Jessie present we tried to control our exuberance. Even Black Sandy was more subdued, though nothing could stop him breaking into song now and again.

At one point I saw him dig Jessie in the ribs. 'What aboot a duet, Jessie wumman?' I heard him suggest. The idea! The rigid figure never relaxed. I could not even hear her stays creak as she sat silently staring at the road ahead.

At intervals Black Sandy drew in at the roadside and deposited his cargo of scholars one by one till Jessie and I were the only two left. We alighted together at the lodge gates at Camptown. Mary-Anne was out feeding her hens with corn held in her apron.

'Daursay! are you gettin' lairnt at the schule noo, Jessie?' she asked with a rare display of humour; but she did not wait for an answer, being too preoccupied with a black Minorca whose feathers were drooping.

'Puir wee Minnie's no' hersel'. Doon in the pook. I'll need to tak' her into the hoose an' set her on the rug.'

Out of the corner of my eye I saw Big Bob scuttling through the hedge. He would never dare show himself with Jessie around. Good riddance!

The two of us walked down the road together in silence. I could not think of a conversation to start with her, there was such a withdrawn look on Jessie's face. And so we came to the parting of the ways at the farm road-end, she to continue round to the herd's hoose, I to climb up the brae towards the farmhouse.

I hesitated before leaving her, not wanting to loosen the chord.

'Ta-ta, Jessie.'

She paused and fumbled in her shabby reticule. I noticed that the flowers were missing, but that there were a few packages there, purchases she had made in town. She took one out and handed it to me. A bag of jujubes.

'Oh, thanks, Jessie!'

So she had not forgotten me during her solitary pilgrimage.

Emboldened, I asked her, 'Are you coming in tomorrow?'

'What for no'?' said she, as if there had never been any doubt about it, and turned away. So that was all right. A load was lifted off my shoulders, and the jujubes tasted all the better as I chewed my way up the brae.

She was in next morning as if nothing had happened, and everything was back to normal. But not a word of explanation, nor did I ever solve the mystery. I could have gone, I suppose, to the abbey churchyard to see if I could find the grave on which she had left the flowers, but I never did.

It was Jessie's secret, whatever it was. And so it remains.

13. Once Upon a Time

It was the most important day of my life, I suppose, the day
of the broadcast. It had crept nearer and nearer, crept as
slowly as a snail, but now it was here. This was the day. My
day.

So far I had kept it to myself. The secret was burning a
hole in my schoolbag where no one ever looked except
myself. I had tucked the letter from the BBC inside the
brown paper cover of my algebra book.

We all covered our schoolbooks carefully so that they
could be handed down to other members of the family.
Poor Dumpling! to fall heir to such treasures. Tidy enough
on the outside, but full of scribbles, smudges, and cries of
despair inside. Tommy-rot! I'm fed *up*! Miss Crichton is
a. . . . Heavily scored out in case Miss C's beady eyes lit on
the compliment.

Now that the day had come I wondered if I ought to
share my secret and announce to the family what was
seething inside me. What would their reaction be? Admiration! Astonishment! Disbelief! Or just indifference?

Perhaps I should wait till the actual broadcast and then say, 'Wheesht! Listen to this! It's mine!'

It was Saturday, an ordinary enough day to everyone else, it seemed. Jessie, transformed into a bondager, was out working in the fields, the servant lassie had walked away home for her day off, and I had to fill in the gap by performing various domestic duties. They would help to pass the long hours stretching ahead till five o'clock when *Children's Hour* came on the air.

Think of it! Hundreds, maybe thousands of folk all listening in to *my* story. No wonder I had the collywobbles. It seemed the only and most important event happening in the world that day.

But it wasn't.

I was at the table with Father who was eating his breakfast in a daze, helping to feed the smaller fry. I had already given my toddling brother his porridge. He was now sitting on the floor pretending to read the *Squeaker* though it was upside down, leaving me to concentrate on coaxing the Dumpling to take some nourishment. He thought it was a game and kept knocking the spoon out of my hand.

'Come on, you! Open your mouth! One for the pussy cat! That's right! Swallow! No! don't spit! One for the pet lamb. Come *on*! Open!'

'Boof!' said the Dumpling, bespattering me with porridge.

It was all part of the ritual of feeding time.

I sometimes wondered what would happen if we just left the Dumpling alone. Would he starve, or crawl his way to the cupboard and chew up paperbags full of sugar? The beasts in the fields had a better way of fending for themselves.

'Another! One for Flora the pony,' I was saying patiently when Mother came through from the hall where she had been answering the telephone. We could tell by the excited look on her face she had a titbit of news to impart.

She made the most of it like an actress taking the centre of the stage, hanging on to her news to keep us on tenterhooks rather than blurting it out straight away.

Her face was slightly flushed and I could see how attractive she looked, even in her workaday blouse and skirt, with her hair escaping untidily from its pins.

'You'll never guess!' she said dramatically.

We tried.

'Bella at the post office has the measles,' I suggested, fending off the Dumpling's attempts to plaster me with porridge.

'Tuts!' said Mother, dismissing the measles. It was better than that.

Father, finishing off his breakfast cup of tea, gave a comical lift to his eyebrows.

'I know! We've been invited to Buckingham Palace for the weekend.'

He was often there himself in his dreams, when his funnybone seemed to work overtime.

'Nonsense!'

Mother gave him a reproving look, then keeked in the kitchen mirror, admiring herself in her role as leading lady. She tidied a stray strand of hair before making her announcement.

'They're on their way!'

'Who?' we asked.

The answer deflated me to such an extent I almost hit the Dumpling with the porridge spoon.

It was *them*! That lot! My elder brother and sister, unexpectedly coming home from their colleges in Edinburgh for the weekend. I would sooner it had been the measles.

Father was pleased, Mother delighted. They would go in to Jedburgh later on to meet the train. Meantime, hustling and bustling plans had to be made, all concentrated on *them*.

'I'll need to do a baking,' said Mother, rolling up her

sleeves, the actress giving way to the practical housewife as she figured out menus in her mind.

'Apple tart. Trifle. There's plenty of cream; they like that. And what about a chicken to roast?'

'I'll see to it,' said Father, rising to his feet.

We had no deep freeze but there was always instant food on the farm, though it meant sacrificing some poor creature's life to make a feast for unexpected guests. Poor chicken!

'Stop it!' I said crossly, wiping the porridge off the Dumpling's face.

The game was over.

I was kept on the go at Mother's command, washing the dishes, helping with the beds, peeling potatoes, whipping cream for the trifle, setting the table. All for *them*. It was doubtful if they would notice my existence or even throw me a word.

But I still had my secret. In the midst of my activity it kept popping back into my head at intervals. I wondered if I might share it with Mother, but it would have little impact compared with the great news that they were coming. Besides, she and Father would be on their way to town by the time *Children's Hour* was on the air.

So I just kept it to myself.

When I had finished my duties I ran out of the kitchen door to get a gulp of fresh air.

One of the hinds – Wull – was on his way round from the work stable leading Prince.

'Where are you going, Wull?' I asked, admiring the horse's powerful body and clumping hooves. Many a ride I had enjoyed on his broad back. It would be nice to have one now.

'I'm awa' to the smiddy. He's needin' a new shoe,' said Wull, patting Prince's sleek side. 'What aboot comin', lassie?'

Why not?

'Hold on a tick,' I cried and ran into the house to ask permission.

Mother was not pleased. She asked me if I had done this, that and the next thing. Had I finished all my tasks?

'Yes, I have, and I won't stay long.'

'You'd better not. Remember you'll have to look after things while your father and I are away to the train.'

'I'll remember. I won't be long.'

'Well, then,' she said reluctantly.

I was off like a shot. I stood on the old mounting stone outside the kitchen door – the loupin' on stane – and Wull gave me a hitch up till I landed safely on Prince's back. It was great, jog-trotting down the road with Wull plodding by my side, occasionally saying, 'W'hup! Steedy, auld horse!'

His wife was shaking the stoor from the rug at the cottage door as we passed. I wondered if she and Wull would exchange greetings. If we had been living in a novelette she would have rushed into his arms. 'William, my dearest, how handsome you look. My heart throbs at the sight of you.'

But she never looked at him at all. Just shook out the rug more vigorously while Wull said another 'W'hup!' and passed by.

The smiddy was by the roadside on the way to Camptown, and the smith – wee Jake Eliot – was not a mighty man; but he was a handyman, carpenter as well as smith, who could mend machinery, build wardrobes, bedsteads or henhouses at the drop of a hammer. He had little to say for himself and no wonder; his mouth always seemed to be full of nails.

Today he was hammering at a big, curiously-shaped box.

'What's that?' I asked, sliding off Prince's back.

Jake shifted some nails with his tongue into the corner of his mouth.

'A coffin,' said he.

'Oh dear!' I said, standing back from it. 'Is somebody dead?'

'Daursay no!' said Jake. 'But I aye like to keep ane ready, just in case.'

As he looked at me, I felt he was measuring me for size.

'A'weel, it's no' coffins we're wantin'. It's shoes,' said Wull, getting down to business.

'Richt!' said Jake, turning his attention to the living. 'Let's see!'

I had watched the performance dozens of times before, but it never failed to fascinate me. Jake hammering at the anvil, the sparks flying, the horse standing patiently on three legs. I was always concerned in case the beast was being hurt.

'No' him! Canna feel a thing,' Jake assured me, fixing a nail into the new shoe. 'Stand steedy!'

When the shoe was firmly in place, Wull lingered for a crack with the smith, which consisted of long silences while the pair of them filled their pipes. I could see they were in for a lengthy session, so, mindful of my duties, I left them to it and hurried home on my own.

As I was passing the hinds' cottages Mrs Thingummy looked out, not with a rug to shake this time. She had one of Wull's thick knitted socks in her hand and was darning a gaping hole in the heel. There was a mouth-watering smell from inside. Spare-ribs, was it? And I could see a batch of freshly baked scones propped up on the table to cool.

'Where's he?' she called out to me.

'Wull? Oh, he's still at the smiddy.'

'Huh! Hingin' aboot bletherin'.'

She jabbed the darning needle into her man's sock as if she was jabbing it into him. I could see her colour rising.

Good! I thought. She's alive, with some human feelings for her man, not just indifference.

'Now you'll remember to do this and that,' Mother admonished me before she and Father set off in the motor.

'Yes, I will.'

And I'll remember to turn on the wireless in good time for *Children's Hour*. As if I would forget!

The time dragged on. The chicken was roasting gently in the oven, the soup bubbling in a pot by the side of the fire, the trifle keeping cool in the milkhouse, the table nicely laid in the dining room. What a fuss to make for that lot!

As the time for the broadcast drew nearer I began to feel restless. Frightened and excited at the same time. I looked up the *Scotsman*. My name was not there. It just said: Story – 'Sandy Squirrel'. My story.

I heard him before I saw him. Yorkie the tramp roaring up the road. He did not bother to thump at the kitchen door. Just came in as if the place belonged to him, sat down by the kitchen table and demanded something to eat.

'Food!' he shouted, sniffing the various appetizing aromas. 'I'm hungry.'

'Right!' I said, not flinching. 'I'll get you something to eat if you go and sit on the bench outside. Out!'

I did not know I had it in me, but it worked. Yorkie gave me a wild look, then rose to his feet and went out muttering angrily to himself. I hastily swung the kettle over the fire, brewed a pot of tea, cut thick slices of bread, spread them with butter and cheese, and added a chunk of leftover mutton, then carried the whole lot out to him. It was the best I could do.

I was trembling. The time which had dragged before was now rapidly ticking nearer and nearer to five o'clock. I rushed through to the parlour to turn on the wireless set, wondering how many folk all over the country would be settling down to listen. Would they announce my name? 'Sandy Squirrel' by Lavinia Derwent.

I turned the knob. Not a sound, not even a crackle of atmospherics. The set was dead. In despair I gave it a kick. Sometimes that did the trick. Not today. The air-waves remained silent.

The grandfather clock in the hall began to wheeze, gathering its breath before it struck five. This did not mean the time was five o'clock. Sometimes it was fast, sometimes slow. Which was it today?

I was beside myself, not knowing what to do, when I heard the herd's dogs barking outside.

'Jock!' I ran out in a frenzy, calling to him. 'Come in!'

'What is't? Man-lassie, ye're in a terrible tizzy. I've been keepin' an eye on *him*,' he said, indicating Yorkie wolfing down his bread and cheese. 'What's up?'

'The wireless. It's not working. Can you come in and sort it?'

'Have ye tried kickin' it?'' inquired the herd, following me through the house to the parlour.

'Yes, I've kicked it.'

Jock kicked it, too, for good measure. Then he remembered.

'Batteries! That's what it's needin'. The Boss was sayin' he wad need to fetch new anes frae the toon. I doot ye'll no' get a squeak oot o't.' Jock gave up. 'Man-lassie, what aboot the grammyphone? Wad ye no' like to play that?'

'No, never mind,' I said, trying to swallow my disappointment. 'It doesn't matter, Jock. Thanks.'

So I never did hear my first broadcast.

If I had been the Carthorse I would have burst into tears. Certainly there was a lump in my throat as I trailed back to the kitchen. The Dumpling was sitting on the rug holding a conversation with Blackie the cat, and the toddler, in a fractious mood, was under the table pulling an old alarum clock to pieces, whining away to himself.

I shushed them both and sat down beside the Dumpling on the rug.

'How would you like me to tell you a story? Listen! Once upon a time there lived a wee Squirrel called Sandy. . . .'

I tried to be pleased to see the Edinburgh pair when they arrived. They were nice enough, but far too full of themselves to take any notice of me. A young lady and gent absorbed in their own activities in the capital city, talking endlessly about tennis matches they had won, exams they had passed, films they had seen, friends they had made.

Father and Mother hung on their words while they sat at their supper, blossoming under all the attention they were receiving. Why should they bother to ask me how I was getting on as I went backwards and forwards with dishes of food to set before them? Nothing could happen to me.

'*She*'ll do the dishes,' said Mother at the end of the meal. 'Sit in by the fire and tell us some more.'

I cleared the table and rattled through the washing-up in a mechanical way, hardly noticing what I was doing. The lump had come back to my throat and the black dog was on my back. The best way to get rid of them both was to go outside for a long walk. Nobody would miss me.

I went through the stackyard. Yorkie was fighting a haystack with his walking stick, like Don Quixote tilting at a windmill.

'Take that!' he bellowed. 'And that! And that!'

For once I felt in tune with him.

Then I saw Jessie. She was making her way home to the herd's hoose, walking wearily after her long day in the fields. I ran after her and fell into step.

She turned and looked at me, noticing at once that the black dog was there. There was no hiding anything from Jessie's direct gaze.

'What's wrang?'

'*They*'re here from Edinburgh for the weekend.'

'Huh!'

Jessie walked on and I walked with her as far as the style which led from the field to the herd's small garden at the back of the house.

Jessie kilted up her skirts to climb over. When she had safely negotiated the style, she said, 'Set them up! Dinna fash, lassie. *You*'ll show them!'

It seemed as if she was backing me against the world. I grabbed her hand, trying to say thank you, but she shook me off.

'Awa' hame, wumman, an' stop feelin' sorry for yoursel'.'

The black dog was sliding off my back as I walked home to the farmhouse with a sprightlier step. I could see the lamplight glowing from the windows of the hinds' cottages, and wondered if Wull was enjoying his spare-rib supper. In the half-light the hills were fading farther away into the distance, but I knew they were there, friendly and sheltering.

And I remembered Robert Louis Stevenson's sad and beautiful poem:

Be it granted me to behold you again in dying,
Hills of home! and to hear the call;
Hear about the graves of the martyrs the peewees crying,
And hear no more at all.

Sad and beautiful. Like life.

But more beautiful than sad, for the farmhouse now seemed to be beckoning me back with its cheerful lights, and when I went in Mother said in a kind voice, 'Come on, lass, we've missed you. Sit down and have a rest. You've had a long hard day.'

And that was the time the tears did come to my eyes.